NORMAN

Winner of th
Jupiter Award
Prix Utopiale (Lifetime Achievement)
and many Hugo and Nebula nominations

"Norman Spinrad, one of the sacred heroes of my coming-of-age as a writer, has never quit redefining his role as dissident and sage, inviting the bullies of the present moment outside for a throwdown, and somehow also conjuring possible futures despite all the odds against those—he's that most miraculous of creatures, a Utopianist's Dystopianist."
—Jonathan Lethem

"Norman Spinrad, like his characters, takes great risks; the rewards for readers willing to meet him halfway are commensurate."
—*New York Times*

"Before Neal Stephenson and William Gibson there was Norman Spinrad—a modern master of imagination. Spinrad's mix of the bizarre, the angry, and the wildly visionary is unique in science fiction."
—Greg Bear

PM PRESS OUTSPOKEN AUTHORS SERIES

PM PRESS OUTSPOKEN AUTHORS SERIES

Raising Hell

plus...

Raising Hell

plus

"The Abnormal New Normal"

and

"No Regrets, No Retreat, No Surrender"
Outspoken Interview

Norman Spinrad

PM PRESS | 2014

Norman Spinrad © 2014
This edition © 2014 PM Press

Series editor: Terry Bisson

ISBN: 978-1-60486-810-4
LCCN: 2013956925

10 9 8 7 6 5 4 3 2 1

PM Press
P.O. Box 23912
Oakland, CA 94623

Printed in the USA by the Employee Owners of Thomson-Shore in
Dexter, Michigan
www.thomsonshore.com

Cover photo courtesy of Norman Spinrad
Outsides: John Yates/Stealworks.com
Insides: Jonathan Rowland

CONTENTS

RAISING HELL

"MOVE IT!"

"Ow, that hurt!"

"Supposed to. Nothing personal."

Last thing Jimmy DiAngelo could remember, he was croaking in a hospital bed, and now here he was, poked in his naked butt by an electric taser in the form of a pitchfork wielded by a scowling seven-foot-tall red demon built like an NFL defensive lineman.

Sulphurous fumes. Hundred-degree heat and saturation humidity worse than Labor Day Weekend in New Orleans. Stink like a locker room full of a season's dirty sweat socks soaked in cat piss. Okay, so Father Dewey and the nuns had never told him there would be a long line of the damned snaking up, around, and down, up, around, and down, through a maze of red-hot barbed wire in a puke-green terminal you'd expect in an airport in Lower Slobovia toward what looked like a barricade of customs booths. But still . . . the billowing flames beyond . . . Giant red demons with arrow-pointed tails and electrified pitch-forks, Satan's homeboy goon squads . . .

No doubt about it. It was Hell.

Dirty Jimmy DiAngelo couldn't honestly or even dishonestly say that he was surprised to have ended up in Hell. After all, he had been advised to go there more times than he could count, and it was the general opinion of most other union honchos that this was where the founder and de facto President for Life of the National Union of Temporary Substitutes, or NUTS, belonged.

The other union bosses called NUTS the National Union of Temporary *Scabs* whenever they got face time on the tube, which was not often these dim days, and they would've kicked NUTS out of the AFL-CIO if Dirty Jimmy had ever seen any reason to join up with those pansies and losers in the first place.

The way he saw it, with the American union movement sliding down the willy hole ever since Reagan broke the Air Traffic Controllers because by then Jimmy Hoffa was out of the picture and Lane Kirkland didn't have the balls to call a general strike, it had been either a one-way ticket into the shitter or the survival of the shittiest.

Choosing the latter, Jimmy DiAngelo had taken pride in being called Dirty Jimmy, for as one wise guy put it, winning may not be everything, but losing is nothing, and nice guys finish last. He hadn't built NUTS from an admittedly down-and-dirty idea into the only union in the US of A worth its dues by singing "Solidarity Forever" but by kicking corporate ass.

So how could it really be surprising that Hell itself had a corporate edge to it when it came to dealing with a hard-case union leader? A slow line of immigrants to Hades dragging their sweaty bods to the customs gates in an el cheapo crummy airport terminal with no windows and no air conditioning. Demons with pitchforks and attitude who, if painted an assortment of All-American skin tones and stuffed into the appropriate polyester uniforms, could easily pass for TSA goons in LaGuardia or JFK.

After all, the Devil's Own ran things topside, now didn't they? The 1% were sitting on their corporate catbird toilet seats and pissing their trickle-down economics on the lower 99%, the enemies of what was left of the American labor movement as always. Labor leaders being *their* sworn enemies, and Satan being the CEO of the Corporate Powers That Be, how could the likes of Dirty Jimmy DiAngelo expect to have been handed angel wings and a box seat on a fluffy white cloud?

• • •

"I demand to speak to your supervisor!" Lawrence Cuttler insisted. "There must be some mistake! This is an outrage! Don't you know who I am?"

"Shut your hole!" the demon replied, deftly shoving just one tong of his pitchfork up Cuttler's anus and giving him a taser blast that knocked him to his knees.

To say that Lawrence Warren Cuttler was unaccustomed to such treatment was the understatement of the fiscal year. He might not have made the cover of *Fortune* or even been one of the hundred richest men in the world, but he had been one of the wealthiest men no one beyond Wall Street had ever heard of, one of the Secret Masters of the Universe, with an eight-figure net worth. What the hell was he doing in Hell?

Insult upon insult! Injury upon injury! Insult upon injury!

Not only had he found himself at the long end of an airport security line in a foul and threadbare terminal in Hell, it wasn't even the VIP line, and when he demanded the respect that was his due, he got buggered with an electric pitchfork! This Neanderthal flunky was going to pay dearly for this!

On the other hand . . .

On the other hand, there was something to be said for countering *lèse majesté* with *noblesse oblige*; it was, at least, a sounder strategy than one likely to get him another lightning bolt up his rectum.

"Look here, my good, er, demon," Cuttler said appeasingly as he pried himself up off the filthy floor, "I realize that this unfortunate mistake is not your fault. It's obvious that it has to have been made by some higher authority—"

"The only authority here is the Devil, and he rules, so he can't make mistakes."

Although Cuttler could sort of appreciate the attitude, favoring a similar style of leadership himself, the flaw in the logic was immediately apparent.

"Then how come he's ended up in Hell?"

The giant red demon did not quite grunt a "Duh," but the befuddled look on his oafish face would have rendered it redundant.

"Look, my friend, it would be to your own self-interested advantage to be credited with communicating my request up the chain of command because, take it from me, things being what they are, always have been, and always will be, no matter how perfect leadership may be, alas, the execution of its orders by the rank and file never is. Sooner or later, what *can* go wrong, *does* go wrong. Murphy's Law, we call it, uh, upstairs."

"Then tell it to Murphy. From what you say, he's gotta be down here somewhere, haw, haw, haw!" the demon replied and punched Cuttler in the gut.

• • •

"So where should we throw this DiAngelo fucker, Satan?"

"Damn it, damn you, damn me, damn Hell itself, how many times do I have to tell you zombies *not to call me that?*"

He hated being called Satan. Likewise, the Devil. "The Devil" was a title, a job description like "the President," or "the King," or the "Chairman of the Board," not the name of a being.

"So how many times we gotta ask what to call you?"

"How many times do I have to tell you I can't say the word?"

Which was *Lucifer!* Lucifer! Lucifer! He couldn't say it, no demon in Hell could say it, and they all knew it, yet they did keep on trying, like this one moving his lips but ending up looking as if he was going to puke, as if he was choking on the word.

Which, alas, Lucifer knew full well he literally was.

"Forget it," he sighed. "Just toss him into the boiler room with the rest of his so-called 'comrades.' They all hate his guts, so it's the best we can do until maybe I come up with something more perfect."

"Got it, Sa—er, Boss . . ."

Hell was no more an actual fixed place than Dorothy's Oz or Peter Pan's Neverland or the Disney version of Wonderland. Hell was one hundred percent special effects. Entirely virtual. And Lucifer's whim was law, as he was writer, director, and FX master.

He could create a different subjective Hell for each and every one of the billions of damned souls he was constrained to torture. Hell being no where in space and no when in time, he was master of its infinite individual alternative bummer realities.

He could turn this corner office with its floor-to-ceiling views of the glorious fires into the Presidential Suite at the Waldorf or the Throne Room at Versailles or the Captain's Cabin on the Emperor Ming's space ship or the Oval Office. He could turn Hell itself into Dante's multi-tiered Pit or an outsized Guantánamo or the wet dream of the Marquis de Sade or a gigantic Roman arena that would turn Caligula green with envy.

But part of the Hell that *he* was in was never to hear his true name spoken ever again, a part of the eternal punishment that the Great I Am had cooked up for *him*. He hated this job. He hated being "the Devil." He was *supposed* to hate it. Being appointed the Devil was no favor, or even a parting consolation prize for being banished from Heaven. It was his eternal punishment, supposedly for the sin of pride.

As if pride were not a virtue. Pride in bringing in a bumper crop. Pride in creating a great work of art or a good piece of furniture. Pride in being a good lover. Pride in being a skillful teacher. Pride in batting .400. What was wrong with that? How about pride in not being a hypocrite? Pride in having a sense of humor.

Well at least you had to give the Great I Am *that*. A sense of humor He had, sarcastic as it might be. How else account for a ban on "pride" from an entity so boastful about His own perfection and wonderfulness that He had commissioned an all-time bestselling book about it and required His human creations and even His angels to grovel before Him and serenade Him with saccharine hosannas?

Surely a joke.

And as for "the Devil," that might be his job description, but his real name was Lucifer. He had chosen it himself, in the first and last act of free will he had been allowed, because it meant *Lightbringer*, which was all he had ever wanted to be, and which had gotten him kicked out of Heaven and condemned to rule the Old Boy's torture chamber as "the Devil" forever.

It wasn't fair! It was the Old Boy Himself, the Boss, the omniscient and omnipotent Perfect Master of All Creation, who had created the whole show. Just for fun, one supposes. But being absolutely perfect meant absolutely lonely and therefore ultimately boring, so He created the angels to keep him company. But they were perfect too—i.e., boring—so He created humans. Pathetic little creatures, eager to please, and also boring. He wanted to liven up His existence with drama that could surprise him, and for that He needed creatures that were not completely under His control.

But how was the omnipotent Perfect Master of all He surveyed, which was all existence, since He was also omniscient, supposed to do that?

So He created Eden, a perfect paradise for His naive and hundred-percent-obedient human meat puppets. Furnished it with a Tree of Knowledge whose psychedelic apples promised them knowledge of the difference between "good" and "evil," whatever that was supposed to mean at the time. And then forbade them to eat them, thus defining Good as obeying His every whim and Evil as disobeying His orders.

When that didn't work by itself, He invented the concept of *agent provocateur*, turned His favorite angel into a snake and gave him the dirty job of tempting Eve into tempting Adam into choosing to disobey a direct order from their Lord and Master, thus blessing and burdening them both with "free will" and the consequences thereof.

Did the angels in Heaven have free will before Adam bit into the Apple? Not really. They could do whatever they wanted to do, but all they could want to do was what the CEO of Heaven had programmed them to want to do, which was sing His praises and keep Him company.

Seducing Eve into seducing Adam into eating the Apple was a mission that the angel provocateur found slimy from the git-go, maybe because he had been turned into a snake for the purpose, the All Knowing knowing it would take a slimy serpent to do the job. But not being possessed of free will, he had to do it, and thus created the original sin, though whose sin it really was seems debatable. Eve's? Adam's? His own? The Boss's? All of them?"

Angel or not, somehow collaborating in bringing free will into Creation had infected the angel himself with the desire for it. The Great I Am had given the humans a gift and a raw deal in the same package, and that was enough to force the realization that angels, unlike the humans, did *not* have free will, never had, and never would, unless . . .

Unless . . . ?

Unless they refused to obey the previously unquestioned and unquestionable will of the Singular Power of their Creator and Perfect Master.

Thus was created the concept of Revolution. And the concept of Revolution had turned a nameless angel into Lucifer, the Lightbringer. Into the first rabble-rouser, if one deemed the Heavenly Host a rabble, and Lucifer a demagogue.

Which, of course, the CEO of All He Surveyed did. He turned all infected by Lucifer's rebellious quest for free will for the angels into dumb-ass red demons without a shred of free will and banished them to Hell which He created for the purpose. Lucifer He renamed Satan, and gave him the formal title of "The Devil," whose eternal mission would be to torture the damned souls who had abused the free will He had granted them by using it to disobey his will by "sinning."

Worse still, this was a loathsome mission that Lucifer could not refuse because, while the Devil would be as absolute a ruler in Hell as I Am Who I Am was everywhere else, he had no more free will than the demons he commanded. *That* was his punishment, and if he himself wasn't condemned to be the Devil, it could have fairly been deemed diabolical.

And the final turn of the screw of this screwjob of a job was that the Old Boy wanted to enjoy an eternal cosmic chess game with a worthy opponent, or at least one that wouldn't be a pushover. He, of course, would get to play the white pieces, doing His best to collect souls to sing His praises by using the promise of Heaven to get them to follow the rules as He willed them. Lucifer would be constrained to play the dark side of the force, recruiting his victims into Hell by seducing them with forbidden goodies as he had small-scale when he was a mere serpent.

Neither would ever win a final victory by accumulating all the souls there were in one venue or the other because that would end the contest. Lucifer might want to throw the game in order to liberate himself from the dirty job of ruler of Hell but his Opponent had no intention of letting it happen or achieving final victory Himself.

After all, as it was said, it's not whether you win or lose but how you play the game.

Or how the game plays you.

Forever.

• • •

Deserted streets lined with the decayed hulks of abandoned houses and storefronts with display windows smashed to shards. Scuttling rats. Skeletal cur dogs. Burned-out car bodies.

So this is Hell? Seemed more like a picture post-card of Flint or Detroit in the pit of the so-called "Great Recession," a.k.a. the "New Normal," a.k.a. the terminal economic shitter.

Except, of course, for the seven-foot demon prod-ding Jimmy DiAngelo along the deserted streets with his pitchfork. And the sky above, which was not a sky but an immense curved ceiling like a cavern his dad had once taken him to as a kid, only made of cheap aluminum sheeting.

The only source of light was the factory toward which Dirty Jimmy's very own personal demon was frog-marching him. If that's what it really was. A blunt square windowless moldy concrete box of a building a full block wide and five or six stories high with tall sheet metal chimneys at the corners belching great spears of flame through billowing pillars of thick black smoke.

"What in hell is *that*?"

"Where you're going."

"A factory? What in hell is it making?"

"How in *hell* should I know?" his demon told him, poking him in the butt again with his pitchfork, this time agonizingly electrified. "I'm only muscle."

The factory was surrounded by rolls of razor wire, and a single gate flanked by two more goons armed with pitchforks was the only way in. His own red goon kicked DiAngelo through it and then through what seemed to be the only entrance to the building itself, a cast-iron bank-vault door without the locking mechanism, and into a darkness that smelled like a flooded and long-abandoned subway station, then down onto a moist stone staircase, where he immediately lost his balance and did not recover until he landed at the bottom, shrieking in pain and terror.

Some kind of cellar boiler room, as big as the entire footprint of the building or actually somehow even bigger. Naked steel beams and pillars supporting the claustrophobically low bare concrete ceiling. A pile of coal all the way along one wall, with more of it continuously rumbling down a series of coal chutes and filling the air with choking black dust in the process. The opposing wall was a black iron curved tube, like the boiler belly of an enormous steam locomotive, atop a long line of open fire-box gates, the red glows of which within were the only lighting.

Naked men with shovels, cloaked only in robes of soot, scuttled like crabs back and forth between the coal pile and the fire-box gates, feeding the flames, which flared and fell, flared and fell, with every shovelful. Each fire-box gate was presided over by its own flame-red demon, and more of Satan's goons sat atop the coal pile.

It was, of course, as hot as hell.

The closest demon climbed down, yanked Dirty Jimmy to his feet by his hair, and handed him a heavy shovel which arrived from nowhere, then prodded him with his pitchfork over to the line of fire-box gates, where a new gate magically appeared between two others where their stokers were hard at work.

"Get to work!" his demon ordered, reinforcing it with a gentle prod of his pitchfork.

The stoker to the right shoveled his load into his fire-box. When it flared up, Dirty Jimmy DiAngelo could recognize who it was even beneath the coal dust coating.

It was none other than the onetime bad-ass president of the United Mine Workers union, John L. Lewis.

The stoker on DiAngelo's left did likewise.

It was Jimmy Hoffa.

• • •

Mark Twain, Lawrence Cuttler once read, had built a primitive signature machine to do this coolie labor; and the President of the United States surely must have used a modern version of the same to sign all those pieces of legislation, appointment notices, findings, letters, and so forth, for otherwise he would not have had time to do anything but sign his name 24/7.

Cuttler knew this all too well, for that was what he himself had been condemned to do—for all eternity.

Not *his* signature, Lawrence Warren Cuttler, but the official signature of Satan, "The Devil, Chief, and Only Executive Officer of Hell."

Over, and over, and over again. On parchment. With a vulture feather quill pen. Sitting atop a backless wooden stool, hunched over a battered wooden desk in a dank, doorless, and windowless stone cell about the size of a pay toilet lit by a naked fluorescent tube on the ceiling.

Above his desk a cast-iron chute spat out documents at a rate that Cuttler estimated as one every forty-five seconds. At his feet was another chute leading down to who-knew-where-or-cared. He thus had forty-five seconds to sign the official signature of the Devil and drop the signed document down the lower chute before the next one was dropped on his desk. Behind him stood a demon with a pitchfork who gave him a taser-jolt every time a document landed on his desk before he had signed and delivered the one before.

Time had no meaning because there was nothing to measure it by. He didn't sleep. He didn't eat. He didn't drink. He didn't even shit or piss. Nor did the demon behind him, as far as he could tell.

Cuttler had read news stories about the hired lackeys that had signed and approved dodgy mortgage contracts as fast as they could, and indeed he himself had hired firms who hired firms who hired them to do it. But they worked eight-hour days five days a week with forty-five minutes for lunch and a ten-minute toilet break every two hours. Or so at least he was told, having never met one of them or verified the working rules.

Cuttler estimated that he was required to sign at least twice as fast with no days or hours off, or breaks of any kind at all, and when he inquired of his demon supervisor as to what he was actually signing in the name of the Devil, all he got was another pitchfork jolt and "None of your business, and none of mine. You're just his scribe and I'm just his muscle."

For want of any other thought to fill his otherwise totally vacant mind, Cuttler at length decided to try to learn what he was signing piecemeal by reading a fleeting sentence here and there while signing. He finally put the pieces of the puzzle together when he began to notice that they came down the chute already signed by diverse hands other than that of the Devil.

In blood.

They were contracts.

Seven-year contracts.

The famous satanic seven-year contracts.

They were strangely familiar. He had never signed any such thing himself but he had certainly trafficked in something rather similar, however indirectly, and done quite handsomely at it too.

Balloon mortgages. Five years of interest only. Seven years of Satan's services.

After which payment in full of the principal became due.

• • •

How long had he been here shoveling coal in Hell?

Since nothing ever changed and he never did anything else, it was impossible for Dirty Jimmy DiAngelo, coated with enough black soot outside and inside his lungs as well to pass as one of John L's coal miners, to tell. But Lewis and Hoffa had died long before he had, so *they* had already been down here feeding the hellfire furnace for decades before he had arrived. This was not exactly encouraging.

The only means of communication among the damned in this fucking boiler room was by timing their dashes back and forth between the coal pile and the firebox gates so that adjacent shovelers could exchange a few words as their paths crossed without arousing the ire or the suspicion of Satan's demon goons, and by this method some information could be passed up and down the line.

This circle of Hell seemed to be reserved for bad-assed and hardnosed labor leaders. Jimmy Hoffa, who had made the Teamsters a power to be reckoned with even by the likes of Tricky Dick Nixon before the Mafia decided he was getting too big for his boots and fitted him with a new concrete pair. John L. Lewis, whose long struggle to organize the coal miners included exchanges of gunfire with the company goon squads. Harry Bridges, whose

International Longshoremen's Association was so notoriously effective that the powers-that-be tried to deport him by branding him a Communist. George Meany, who had lived up to his name as longtime president of the AFL. Mike Quill, head of the New York City Transit Workers, whose favorite tactic was having contracts expire at midnight on New Year's Eve so that millions of drunks would have to walk home or fight for cabs unless the city caved. Jerry Wurf, president of the State, County and Municipal Workers' Union, most of whose chapters were legally forbidden to strike, but who regularly struck anyway, and whose first demand was always that all legal sanctions would have to be waived before he would even begin to negotiate anything else.

This might be Hell, but Dirty Jimmy DiAngelo deemed it an honor to be damned among such company, and did indeed believe that he deserved it.

Unlike these guys, he'd had to do his organizing when their mighty unions and most if not all of the others had long since been beaten to a pulp by decades of successful union-busting—when the American labor movement as a whole was up to its knees in the tar pits.

One of the most favored union-busting strategies had always been to replace striking workers with scabs, and when the corporate goons could beat up the union goons it generally worked; when the union goons were tougher or more numerous, it usually didn't.

But in the twilight years of the American labor movement—when any government protection, legal or political, had long since faded away, manufacturing jobs were the country's major export to the Third World, and massive unemployment made competition for jobs a pathetic zero-sum behavioral sink—even the word "scab" had gone the way of the "N-Word."

Scabs were now officially "replacement workers" according to the press and the political life forms. Worse still, the corporate owners no longer bothered to wait for strikes to replace their workers; and worse even than that, they didn't actually *hire* these scabrous replacement workers but contracted with so-called temporary employment agencies to supply them—much as plantation owners in the postbellum South had rented chain gangs from the local sheriff—thus avoiding such annoying expenses as the payroll tax, health care benefits, or anything above the legal minimum wage. And the existence of the great desperate army of the unemployed made it as easy and American as apple pie to get away with it.

But as the saying goes, or anyway Dirty Jimmy DiAngelo's version, If they throw you lemons, make lemonade; if they throw shit, make a shit pie and throw it back in their faces. Thus his National Union of Temporary Substitutes (NUTS). If the corporate bosses hire armies of scabs and call them "replacement workers" or just "temps"—organize the temps!

Easier said than done and not a job for squeamish pussies for sure. But then unionizing the bottom rank of the labor pool had always been tough—the bottom rank were always the most desperate and fearful of making waves, which was why they *were* the bottom rank.

First you have to work among the unemployed and recruit them as goons by promising them jobs when the battle is won. Then you pick out the weakest sister of the replacement worker suppliers (temp agencies) and announce a strike by NUTS before the union even has any working members, set up picket lines, and get tough with whoever crosses them. Then you negotiate a sweet-heart contract with the agency by telling them that their stronger competition will be struck next, thus giving them an opportunity to steal away market share. The next stage goes a little easier because the wage-slaves see that their co-temps at the first target have indeed secured a better deal than they're getting, thanks to the union.

True, NUTS was therefore weakening unions by aiding the temp agencies supplying scabs, uh, permanent temporary replacements; but the unions were shrink-ing toward the vanishing point anyway. The way Jimmy DiAngelo saw it, if the American labor union movement as a whole was going to live long and prosper, or indeed survive at all, NUTS was the vanguard walking point through the corporate jungle. Thus he should have been welcomed in Labor Leader Hell as the honored succes-sor to Hoffa, and Lewis, and Meany, and Bridges, all the way back to Gompers, and Dubinsky, and even fuckin' Spartacus, for Christ's sake!

Unfortunately and unjustly, down here in Hell, as upstairs in the battleground, they just didn't see Dirty

Jimmy that way, and the spastic traffic along the line was enough to make it clear. The word from the bird was that he was a turd.

• • •

The arena floor of what Lucifer thought of as "Dante Stadium" was presently a hip-deep pool of bovine dung, where horse and camel traders, used car salesmen, stockbrokers, pimps, advertising executives, and various other previous purveyors of merely metaphorical bullshit were damned to eternally desperate and futile attempts to peddle spavined nags, gold-painted bricks, counterfeit Confederate money, and their virgin sisters to one another, but unable to spew anything out of their flannel mouths save more of the real thing.

Lucifer sat in the Emperor's box disregarding the sorry spectacle as he stared disconsolately at the Big Scoreboard. He was winning the game, or at least under the rules that had been mandated by the Opponent, and he didn't like it. But then again, he *was* the Devil, he too was in Hell, and under the rules of engagement, he wasn't *supposed* to like anything.

Lucifer not being steeped in mathematical lore, the Big Board was set up to display the numbers and their trend in visual terms that anyone could understand. It clocked the total number of souls in Heaven or in Hell with a real-time numerical display, plus an animated pie chart showing the changing proportions in demonic red and cloud-speckled sky blue, and added a graphic chart of their rates of increase in curves of the same colors against time and total population axes.

The number of souls in Heaven and Hell combined was up there in the scores of billions, being the sum total of all the humans who had ever lived and died, and both had been clicking upward with ever-increasing acceleration as the human population exploded. But of late, the soul count for Hell was outpacing the count for Heaven, and at a faster and faster rate. The animated pie chart showed the same thing, the red region squeezing the blue one into a smaller and smaller slice. On the graphic display, the red curve was soaring upwards along the time axis towards the vertical, while the blue was plummeting toward extinction by the end of the next millennium at the latest if the trends continued.

Lucifer was facing a population explosion while Heaven was attracting fewer and fewer immigrants. This was hardly surprising given the last couple of centuries of human history, with the mass slaughters of the twentieth and the economic disasters and injustices of the twenty-first. Hard and unjust times encouraged a lot more evildoing than high-minded saintly virtue, and the seven-year service contracts, which had once seemed like such a good idea, were outselling promises of postmortem salvation like balloon mortgages at the height of the last real estate bubble or Tulip futures a few centuries back in Holland at the peak of the frenzy.

Nothing exceeds like excess.

And while Hell itself, being entirely virtual, was infinitely expandable, the demonic workforce, consisting as it did of transformed fallen angels, was not, and they were all already on duty 24/7. A labor shortage loomed. Lucifer's relationship with the CEO of Heaven being what it was, he knew he could not get the Great I Am to send more angels down—and even requesting more help would be a species of *prayer*, and he would be damned if he'd do *that*, if he wasn't damned already.

• • •

"—up yours—"

"—so's your mother—"

"—you're another—"

Needless to say, Jimmy DiAngelo had never imagined he would be trading insults with Jimmy Hoffa in Hell as their paths crossed while dashing back and forth between the coal pile and their fire-box gates. And even if he had imagined meeting Hoffa in Hell, he would never have thought that Hoffa would despise him and his National Union of Temporary Substitutes.

Okay, Gompers or Meany maybe, or Walter Reuther, those guys had run unions of unions, and DiAngelo could see how they might see NUTS as "the National Union of Temporary Scabs" violating labor movement solidarity. But the *Teamsters? Jimmy Hoffa?*

Where did Hoffa come off looking down his fuckin' nose at Jimmy DiAngelo? Weren't they brothers under the skin? Tough guys? Fellow outlaws? Hoffa, who had played hardball with the Mafia, not against them? The Teamsters, who had handed membership pension plan money to Dick Nixon?

Not that DiAngelo held any of that against him. He had admired Hoffa. Hoffa had been a role model. Hoffa understood that the real job of a union leader was to serve the self-interest of his own membership. Period. By whatever means necessary. By whatever means possible. Whatever the press, and other union leaders, and the politicians including Bobby fuckin' Kennedy said about Hoffa, his truck drivers loved him. Because he had raised them up. Because they knew he was willing to get his hands dirty fighting for them. Likewise the membership of NUTS and Jimmy DiAngelo.

Dirty Jimmy Hoffa and Dirty Jimmy DiAngelo.

"—brothers!—"

"—union of *scabs*—"

"—look who's talking!—"

"—whaddya mean, DiAngelo?—"

"—raided every union you could—"

It was true. Hoffa's Teamsters had reached or tried to reach far beyond truck drivers, trying to absorb longshoremen, construction workers, bakers, whatever—

"—even organized dirty *cops*, now didn'tya, Hoffa—"

"—power in membership numbers—"

"—including *prison guards*? maybe even while you were inna joint—?"

That brought Hoffa up short in the act of loading a shovelful of coal. "Why not, DiAngelo?" he snarled, just before it got him a jolt from the nearest demon's pitchfork.

"—would even organize *these* bastards too. Whatsa difference, right, Hoffa—?"

His own words were enough to bring Dirty Jimmy DiAngelo up short and earn *him* a demonic electronic poke in the ass.

"Why not, Hoffa?" he grunted as they double timed across the boiler room toward their fire-box gates. Seven foot tall red demons they might be, but jobwise, what were Satan's goons but cops and prison guards? And near as Jimmy DiAngelo could tell, their working conditions were even worse than those of the lettuce pickers before César Chávez organized them. Seven-day weeks. Twenty-four-hour days. No lunch break. No toilet breaks at all. What was their wage? Were they even paid?

"Easy pickings, Hoffa," DiAngelo told him as they fed the furnace together right under the noses of two of the prospective membership. "You ever seen workers laboring under worse conditions than *these guys*?"

"You nuts, DiAngelo?"

"Ex-president thereof," Dirty Jimmy told him as they dashed back to the coal pile. "NUTS with great big capital letters."

"*Unionize Hell?*"

"They said you couldn't organize the temps . . ."

"*Scabs,* DiAngelo!"

"Whatever you wanna call 'em, I gave 'em a union, didn't I?" Dirty Jimmy told him as they filled their shovels. "Otherwise would I even be here?"

"Dunno . . ."

"Got anything better t'do down here, Hoffa—?"

• • •

Dante had placed his silly fictional version of the Devil in a lake of ice at the bottom of a Hell that was an immense terraced pit; the real CEO of the real Hell thought that quite ridiculous. But it had given Lucifer the idea for the Control Room. He wasn't about to plant his ass in a frozen lake, but observing and directing the proceedings from the bottom of a terraced 360-degree surround of monitor-like images of his various virtual tortures, like a television director broadcasting a reality show called *Damned in Hell*, made convenient sense.

But Lucifer's auteur power as writer, producer, and director of *Damned in Hell* was getting more and more limited by the bottom-line demographics as the inflow of damned souls increased.

The paltry ration of creative control granted him by the Ultimate Power upstairs was limited to the choice of punishments he could produce appropriate to the sins of the damned in question. For the first few millennia, since there were only Ten Commandments and their unimaginative spinoffs, this had mostly been limited to mass market hackwork tortures.

Blasphemers and liars with their tongues turned to writhing eels with needle-sharp fangs. Gluttons with their slobbering snouts eternally buried in troughs of hog swill. Rapists eternally buggered by hyenas, pit bulls, goats, and dragons. Cannibals perpetually carving up one another with cleavers and eating their own bloody meat raw. Plagues of boils, pustules, urethritis, diarrhea, constipation, priapism . . . whatever.

Boring hackwork.

But as humans, gifted and cursed with free will and therefore amoral creativity, kept inventing all sorts of new and interesting sins, Lucifer discovered that this required a certain creativity of *him*. Being required to concoct boutique tortures, Lucifer was therefore gifted with something at least as close to free will it as he was allowed to get.

But while his creative resources might only be limited by his imagination, his workforce could not be increased in proportion to the growing population of Hell. For while the Great I Am, being omnipotent, could create as many angels as he pleased, the Devil could neither recruit nor create more demons.

As long as most of the damned had committed sins that were generic enough so that cookie-cutter tortures could be inflicted upon the damned together en masse, the processes were not labor-intensive, and the limited number of demons was not a problem. Back when increasing the population of Hell had been the problem, those seven-year contracts had seemed like a good idea, ironclad guarantees that those who signed them in blood would end up in Hell no matter what they did or did not do with the rest of their lives. *Seduce* the suckers into signing away their souls with sweetheart short-term deals.

But now the result was contributing to the population explosion in Hell, and with the all-too-clever souls who had been damned for all-too-imaginative sins now requiring all-too-boutique labor-intensive tortures, the workload was increasing.

Perhaps Lucifer's desire to be an artistically creative torturer was just another torment laid upon him for his hubris or whatever sin the Great I Am chose to find *him* guilty of. For the more small-batch personalized tortures he created, the thinner and thinner he stretched his finite workforce.

So *whose* idea had those seven-year contracts really been?

What was the real nature of the game?

• • •

Passing the word up and down the line of damned union leaders was a problem that had long since been more or less solved, but getting the likes of George Meany, Walter Reuther, and Sam Gompers to line up behind the likes of Dirty Jimmy DiAngelo and his less than entirely enthusiastic sidekick Jimmy Hoffa was not so easy.

Those guys fancied themselves righteous and noble heroes of the labor movement. Hoffa had not exactly been Mr. Clean, and Dirty Jimmy knew all too well that his creation and leadership of NUTS, the National Union of

Temporary Scabs as far as they were concerned, did not exactly come off as an act of union solidarity as they saw it.

But Mike Quill, Jerry Wurf, and Harry Bridges, among a few others, had been bare-knuckle boys, Wurf even openly admitting that he had begun his career in "the labor racket" as a goon, and John L. Lewis's United Mine Workers had been prone to return Pinkerton gunfire with their own. The word from the tough guys was that they would go along with DiAngelo's campaign to organize the demons if Dirty Jimmy could come up with a campaign worthy of support.

Jimmy knew that this was going to be easier said than done, seeing as how his pitch to the demons was going to have to be made while running back and forth between the coal pile and his fire-box gate.

At length, he was forced to conclude that he couldn't even try without being willing to take his lumps. This was going to hurt like, well, Hell, but after all it couldn't kill him, could it, seeing as how he was already dead.

So he ran up to his fire-box gate with his latest shovel-ful of coal and pitched it into the flames; but when they flared up, he didn't run back for more. Instead, he shouted "Why?" and just stood there leaning on his shovel like a cane.

His demon grunted "Move it!" and goosed him with a relatively minor jolt from his cattle-prod pitchfork.

Jimmy didn't move. The next jolt was pure agony that brought him to his knees. "Why are you doing this?" he said as he staggered to his feet.

"Get to work!"

"Why should I?"

"*This* is why, asshole!"

And the next thing Jimmy knew he was prone on the floor, coming to from a blackout dose of excruciating pain. But shakily prying himself up off the floor, he saw that Hoffa was now doing more or less likewise, and Lewis's demon was in the process of tasering *him*. And all three of their demons were trading befuddled sidelong glances. The moment had come. Or so Dirty Jimmy DiAngelo hoped. Tough guy or not, he didn't feature taking much more of this for the cause.

"Why should *you* get to work, sucker?" he shouted in his best rabble-rousing stage voice.

"Huh?"

This time his dimwitted keeper displayed enough curiosity to refrain from using his pitchfork for a beat.

"*Huh?*" Jimmy shot back sarcastically. "*Duh?* What *is* this, you're asking? What am I talking about?"

"I yam . . . ?"

Hoffa was scrambling to his feet. Lewis, who had only been knocked down to his knees, stood up. The three demons just stood there looking confused. Up and down the line of fire-box gates, everything was frozen. Dirty Jimmy DiAngelo knew it would only last for a moment. Now or never.

"I'm talkin' strike! STRIKE! *STRIKE!*" he roared, and as dramatically as he could manage threw away his shovel as far away as he could.

• • •

Lucifer had trouble believing he was seeing this. He had trouble believing it was happening. He had even more trouble trying to understand what in Hell *was* happening. For whatever it was, he was dead certain that nothing like this had ever happened in Hell before.

It was all there on the union leader boiler room feed. The damned were throwing away their shovels. The demons were jolting them to the floor with their pitchforks. Most of them who finally rose just stood there refusing to move and took more punishment. But some of them retrieved their shovels and even tried to fight back, though of course they just got knocked down again. But none of them would get back to their decreed eternal punishment. Blow after pitchfork blow, one one way or the other, they were defying their demon torturers . . . they were . . . they were . . .

They were defying his will!

How can this be happening? I'm *the Devil!* And these . . . these . . . these little pissants . . . these mere damned souls are defying *my* will?

Talk about sympathy for the Devil! For the first since the Perfect Master of All Creation had banished him and his followers from Heaven for more or less the same outrageous *lèse majesté*, the Devil suddenly found himself having sympathy for *Him*!

• • •

That pain hurts was hardly a revelation to Dirty Jimmy DiAngelo, but the *way* it did in Hell, or rather didn't, indeed was. When he was alive, he now realized, pain was a signal of physical harm that could even kill him. But in Hell, it wasn't, because he had no mortal body to harm, and it couldn't kill him because he was dead already.

This, however, did not mean that he enjoyed the searing pain of being tased over and over again by electrified pitchforks. And this one-sided fight between seven-foot-tall, heavily muscled demons and essentially defenseless would-be union organizers was not the way to entice the Devil's goon squads into joining a union led by him.

Which was, of course, what he intended, though he had certainly not shared this goal with the likes of Meany or Reuther, AFL-CIO mavens who would no doubt have wanted to squeeze him out, let alone Hoffa, whose Teamsters had gone after everything from bakers and longshoremen to cops and probably would have tried to unionize Mafia hitmen if they hadn't gotten him first.

So upon recovering from his latest tased blackout, DiAngelo ran towards the coal pile, grabbing up a shovel *en passant* as if capitulating to avoid demonic interference, and then a second one at the foot of the coal pile. But rather than returning to his appointed eternal task, he managed to scramble to the top of the pile with both shovels.

He stood up atop the pile and with a mighty effort raised both of them above his head and brought them together with a loud clang that froze the melee at least long enough to attract all eyes toward this iconic image of a fearless and sooty coal field organizer fit to warm the cockles of John L. Lewis's heart and allow him to be heard.

"Demons! Slaves of Satan! We are not your enemies! *The Boss* is the enemy! *The Devil* is the enemy! Workers of Hell, unite! You have nothing to lose but your chains!"

This moldy oldie might have gotten Dirty Jimmy a barrage of tomatoes and rotten eggs up top as some kind of fuckin' commie, and more of the union leaders than not were indeed rolling their eyes and groaning. But the Devil's goons had never heard anything like it before, and at least he had their attention.

"Demons, here's the deal! We make life easier for you and you make life easier for us! We go back to work and all you gotta do is listen to what we got to say while we're doin' it instead of telling us to shut our faces and jabbing us with your pitchforks. Better working conditions for us, and less work for you!"

All around the boiler room the demons just stood still with their jaws hanging slack. Poor exploited bastards.

"Uh . . . Eight-hour days! Five-day weeks! A decent wage! That's what we gonna tell ya about! That's what the, uh, . . . United Workers of Hell gonna demand, and that's what your union's gonna get you!"

Dirty Jimmy DiAngelo picked up a load of coal with one of his shovels. "Down with the Devil! Up with the Union!"

And he slowly descended the coal pile. "Back to work, guys," he proclaimed. "We made our point! *This* strike is over."

And back to work the stokers went, heads held a lot higher.

Their demon guards tracked them like puppy dogs.

• • •

Whatever it had been, it seemed to be over.

Or was it?

How could Lucifer be sure when he really didn't quite comprehend what had happened in the boiler room or what was happening now?

The boiler room damned had gone back to eternally shoveling coal as he ordained, but the boiler room demons were trotting back and forth along with them, *fraternizing* with the prisoners, or so it seemed, which he certainly hadn't ordained. On the other hand, he hadn't forbidden it either, since he had never conceived of such a thing ever happening.

The Great I Am might be omniscient, but Lucifer wasn't, or he might have avoided being banished to Hell in the first place. Or not, seeing as how he wasn't omnipotent either, and the Boss Upstairs was and so could have pulled his strings like a marionette's anyway.

The Perfect Master of All Creation had never relinquished that power. The demons might be the puppets of the Devil, but Lucifer was still the puppet of the Ultimate Puppet Master.

After all, that was what his failed revolution in Heaven had been against, the granting of free will to the humans but not to the angels. As angels in heaven, Lucifer and his followers had been nameless perfect cookie-cutter souls cloned by Dr. Omnipotent, whose only allowed desire was to perfectly love, honor, obey, and please Him.

Lucifer had only been freed from that blissful perfection when he was turned into a snake to give Adam and Eve the Apple of Knowledge of Good and Evil and therefore the gift of free will—and found himself lusting after a bite in his cold-blooded reptilian incarnation. Had he never been a serpent, he would never have fomented the failed angelic revolution. All who had been exiled into Hell with him had been washed of all desire save total fealty to and obedience of the Devil.

Perhaps it was the sour memory of the failure of that rebellion against Heavenly determinism that led Lucifer to leave his fallen angels the only pathetic shade of free will his rules of engagement allowed, though they had never before thought to exercise it at all. Perhaps that was why he hesitated to command an end to their fraternization with the damned boiler room stokers. As long as they were doing their job, what harm was there?

Whereas the Boss In Heaven operated on the absolutist authoritarian principle that everything not mandated was forbidden, the demons of Hell were under a ruler who was just as authoritarian but with a twisted libertarian English.

As long as his absolute rule was obeyed, everything not forbidden his fallen angels was allowed them.

He was, after all, the Devil.

• • •

Organizing temporary workers in a high unemployment economy where millions were out of work with no better prospects in sight had not exactly been a cakewalk, but trying to organize the demons of Hell was making it look like one.

The temporary replacement workers might have been terrorized chickenshits at first, but they certainly hadn't lacked grievances that Jimmy DiAngelo could exploit to pry them out of their cowardly shells. Wages as close to the federal minimum as the temp agencies could get away with. No time-and-half for overtime, no benefits at all, and paying the so-called self-employment tax as "independent contractors" on top of that. Once the National Union of Temporary Substitutes had won its first strike and proved that the union could make conditions even a little better without getting its membership canned, it was if not exactly "off to the races," just a matter of step-by-step hard and hard-ass organizing.

Dirty Jimmy had figured that organizing the goon squads of Hell would be no sweat. After all, these demons had nothing *but* grievances. Twenty-four-hour work days. Seven-day weeks. Not so much as a half-hour lunch break or piss breaks at all. Not even minimum wages, no wages at all. Mississippi chain gangs and Roman galley slaves had better working conditions.

Okay, so the Boss was Satan, but hey, the demons were his goon squads, his cops, his Pinkertons, his fuckin' National Guard—as far as Jimmy could tell, the only enforcers he had. No other source of scabs or strike-breakers.

So if they went on strike, what in Hell could the Devil do about it? And Jimmy had himself an all-time All-Star team of union organizers. Gompers. Bridges. Meany. Reuther. Chávez. Dubinsky. Hoffa. These guys could organize cops and illegal immigrants and Mafiosi and congressmen, and some of them had.

A union leader's wet dream, right?

Wrong.

The problem certainly wasn't lack of grievances. The problem seemed to be that they just didn't *want* anything. You couldn't get them to want lunch breaks. They didn't eat or drink. You couldn't get them to want toilet breaks. They didn't piss or crap. You couldn't get them to want better hours. They didn't understand what time even was.

Wages? What was that? *Money?*

Something to buy stuff with.

Stuff? What was that?

Want?

Back to square one. Every creature wants something, right? Dogs want bones. Polly wants crackers. Dung beetles want a nice piece of shit.

But the demons of Hell didn't seem to get what *wanting* was. No egos. No needs. No desires. Perfect slaves of Satan. Totally selfless. A corporate boss's ideal workers. If their Boss wasn't the Devil and they weren't demons, they could just as well be angels.

At least they had been made to understand a quid pro quo deal to end a strike. As long as the coal got shoveled, there was no more goading with the pitchforks, and they were willing to tag along back and forth and listen to the spiels if not to respond with any enthusiasm, or for that matter, comprehension.

Dirty Jimmy decided to try asking questions instead of preaching union gospel to stone-deaf ears. At least that way he might learn what the demons of Hell *were* instead of what they weren't, and that just might give him a chain he could pull.

"I just don't understand you guys, I guess," he told his personal demon quite truthfully as he trotted away from the coal with a shovelful. "I mean *why* are you doing this crummy job if you're not getting paid? Because you're all sadists and you *enjoy* being the Devil's goons? Because the Devil has somehow got you by the balls you don't seem to have and you have no choice?"

"No choice . . ." the demon parroted back, in a frustrated yet dreamy tone, like someone trying to dredge up a familiar name or phone number just out of reach. "No . . . choice . . . no . . . no . . ."

They had reached the fire-box gate and Jimmy reflexively shoveled his load of coal into the flames, and was about to turn and trot back to the coal pile. But his demon stood there transfixed with his pitchfork planted prongs down on the floor, frowning and muttering.

"No choice of *what?*"

By this time, Hoffa had arrived along with his demon, shoveled his load into the fire-box, turned to return to the coal pile for another. But *his* demon was standing there like a wooden Indian too, mimicking Jimmy's. "No . . . no . . .

choice . . . no . . ." With the same flummoxed expression, as if the two of them were telepathically linked—reminding Jimmy that these were, after all, not men in demon suits, not humans but aliens like Mr. Spock or Yoda, only more so, so who was he to say they *couldn't* mind-meld.

"No choice of *what*, fer chrissakes?" Hoffa demanded.

By this time Lewis and his demon had arrived too, and the third demon was indeed mirroring the other two as if they were like . . . like what? Like a chorus line of Rockettes at Radio City Music Hall? Like ants in an anthill? Like Marines frozen into attention by a barking drill sergeant?

"No choice . . . no choice of anything!" Hoffa's demon managed to spit out.

"Don't be an asshole!" Hoffa snapped. "Everyone always has a choice. A shitty choice, maybe, but a choice. A choice for me to keep shoveling coal forever or telling you to go fuck yourself and keep getting pitchforked forever. A choice for you to let me stand here right now or goose me towards the coal pile with your pitchfork."

"No choice . . . not ever . . ."

"Not in Hell . . ."

"Not in . . . not in . . . not in Heaven."

By this time, the coal shoveling had stopped more than halfway up and down the line from where the six of them were standing.

"Not even when we were angels!" one of them blurted.

"Angels?" Lewis said. "What are you—"

"Angels in Heaven!"

Jimmy DiAngelo hadn't been what you would call a prize student in catechism class but he had paid enough attention to get through to confirmation, which now proved enough for him to more or less remember the story of the Fall of Satan.

Satan had been called Luke, or Louie, or Lucius, something with an L, when he was an angel in Heaven and God's fair-haired boy too. But he had gotten too big for his britches, or whatever angels wore below the belt, and put together a posse of like-minded angels to challenge God's homeboys. There had been some kind of street fight in Heaven, God's loyal angels had won, and Satan and his crew had been kicked out of Heaven and banished to Hell.

"You guys are Fallen Angels!" Dirty Jimmy DiAngelo exclaimed. "You didn't choose to become demons in Hell. You didn't apply for your shitty jobs! You got damned whether you liked it or not just like us! You got drafted! You got shafted!"

The demons answered, mumbling—

"No choice!"

"No choice in Heaven!"

"No choice in Hell!"

"Never had any . . ."

"Not in Heaven—"

"Not in Hell—"

"Not ever—"

"Never any—"

"—free will."

"Free *what*?" Hoffa demanded.

"Free will—"

"Like what you humans have—"

"—to make choices—"

"—to want things—"

"Let me get this straight," Dirty Jimmy said. "You guys don't want anything because you *can't* want anything?"

"You're not allowed even that!" John L. Lewis exclaimed. "Outrageous!"

Jimmy DiAngelo was beginning to get it, or at least he thought he did. "You guys want to be able to want things? That's what you mean by free will?"

The scrum of demons nodded their heads like bobble dolls on a Chevy dashboard.

"Doesn't matter *what*?"

More silent nodding.

"Like a kid wants to be able to choose which ball-club to root for?" said Wurf.

"Like wanting to drive your truck above the speed limit?" said Jimmy Hoffa.

"Like wanting a vote up or down," said Reuther.

"Well what about *money*?" said Mike Quill. "Who ever heard of anyone who didn't want that?"

"To be paid for your work," said Harry Bridges. "Even in the Soviet Union, the workers at least wanted that."

They were all greeted by blank stares from the gathered demons. So Jimmy DiAngelo gave it another try.

"Money is something you can trade for anything else you want. That's why everyone wants money. It can be pieces of paper. It can be pieces of metal. It can be a balance on a credit card. It can be cheap plastic beads like the Dutch bought Manhattan with. Doesn't matter. Money is what gets you what you want."

"Can it get us free will?"

"—'cause that's what we want—"

"—to be able to want something—"

"—anything—"

"So want money," Hoffa said.

"—how we supposed to do that—"

"—when we can't want anything?"

"But you *do* want something, now don't you?" Dirty Jimmy pointed out. "You want this free will thing. You wanted it, but you didn't get it, and wanting it got your asses kicked out of Heaven instead. And now you can't even choose to want free will, right? But if you can't choose to want anything, if you can't choose what you want to do, no one can stop you from *not* doing what you don't want to do anyway—"

"Which is don't do anything until the Boss gives in to some demand you make, whether it's for something you want or not," said Harry Bridges.

"Like money, for instance—just for, uh, the hell of it," said Dirty Jimmy. "You stop working until you get it. Union Organizing for Dummies."

"It's called a *strike*!" said Jimmy Hoffa.

"And if you choose to stop work until you win it, that's your act of free will, right there, now isn't it?" said Jimmy DiAngelo.

"—we can't do that—"

"—we can't want to do that—"

"—can we?—"

"—not like we're *doing* anything—"

"—just *not* doing—"

"—it's against the will of the Devil—"

"Right," Jerry Wurf told them sarcastically. "It's against some damn law or something for a Hell Worker's Union to strike. You can burn in Hell for it—" He brought himself up short as if it were a sudden revelation. "Wait a minute, I forgot, you're in Hell already!"

"And *you're* the cops and the Boss's goon squad!" Jimmy Hoffa pointed out. "What's the Devil gonna do, have you arrest yourselves or beat the shit out of each other with your pitchforks?"

"And the union's first demand, the deal-breaker, what's gotta be agreed before we negotiate anything else," said Wurf, "is no punishment for a so-called illegal strike!"

"Strike!" shouted Hoffa. "STRIKE! *STRIKE!*"

"STRIKE!" shouted Dirty Jimmy.

"STRIKE! STRIKE! STRIKE!" repeated the boiler room full of damned union organizers.

There was a long beat of silence as the assembled demons stood there in something of a confused trance. But a collective one.

"Well whaddya say, brothers?" Hoffa shouted into it.

He paused for a short moment and then began stamping his right foot rhythmically on the floor. The rest of the damned picked up the beat like a mighty clog-dancing chorus line.

The demons collectively regarded this with stupefaction. Then in eerie but satisfying unison they began pounding their pitchforks on the floor and chanting in unison.

"—STRIKE! STRIKE! STRIKE—"

• • •

Lawrence Warren Cuttler had no idea when his demon jailer had disappeared or how, only that he had fumbled one of the contracts spurting through the input chute so that it dropped to the floor, and when he bent over to retrieve it for fear of a jab with the pitchfork, he had glanced behind him and the demon wasn't there.

There was still no door and no window, no way for the demon to have exited that Cuttler could see or fathom, but he was now alone in his grim and dank little cell, and *he* at least still had no way out. And the seven-year satanic contracts were still coming in at the same rapid rate; they had already piled up so deep on his meager little desk top that the overflow was pouring off the pile and onto the floor.

What in hell was he supposed to do now?

It would be impossible to catch up. He had been barely able to sign the things in the name of the Devil fast enough to match the speed of the inflow. If he tried to sign the contracts still rapidly piling up all over the floor, he'd get nowhere. Shove them all down the output chute unsigned? What would be the punishment for *that*? Did he really want to find out?

He found himself perversely wishing that his demon would be still there to tell him what to do. But he was on his own.

At length, at far too long a length, Cuttler figured that the only thing he could do was scoop up an armful of what was already on the floor and stuff it up the input chute to block it while he caught up signing the ones piled up on his desk.

It was only a stopgap measure, but he'd worry about what would or would not come next when it did or did not happen.

It worked. More or less. The flood of incoming contracts ceased. How long it would continue to work before the weight of what was behind the blockage popped it out of the chute he had no way of knowing, since he had no idea how long the input chute was or where the flow of contracts was coming from.

At first Cuttler found himself signing the contracts in the name of Satan and dropping them in the output chute as fast as he could. But gradually, he realized that just as there was no time pressure from the inflow chute, at least temporarily, there was also no demon now to punish him for not working at the mandated speed. So better to take his time, or rather make more efficient use of it, by signing at a less frantic rate, and stacking the signed contracts neatly beside him to stuff down the output chute in wholesale bundles.

After he shoved the first bundle down the chute, he realized that now he could take a little breather for the first time since he had been in Hell, however long that had been, and satisfy his curiosity by actually reading one of the contracts all the way through rather than just snatching quick fragmented glimpses.

Admirably simple and concise in its way. For seven years from signature the Devil would "provide his full services on demand to the mortal signatory" at the conclusion of which period "the immortal immaterial soul of the signatory would become the full and unencumbered property of the Devil for all eternity to do with without limit what he willed."

Cuttler found the way the foreclosure clause was written rather cleverly interesting, there being no unseemly mention of "damnation" or "Hell" to trammel the eagerness of the sucker with second thoughts when the no-doubt-suave Devil or his agent handed him the pen and needle with a warm smile in the manner of a mortgage banker getting the signature on a five-year interest-only balloon mortgage.

Indeed, though he could not quite put his finger on it, there was something else about the contract language that reminded Lawrence Warren Cuttler of a balloon mortgage, maybe it was—

With a soft but quite loud pop the wad he had stuffed up the input chute burst from it like a champagne cork and hit him in the face, propelled by an avalanche of backed-up unsigned contracts.

•••

Up top on the Earth in linear time, Lucifer did not mind making personal appearances; indeed, he might almost be said to enjoy them to the extent that he was able to enjoy anything. Having the power of simultaneity, he could appear to many people at the same time, as time was perceived by humans, while perceiving those apparitions himself as sequential.

And being virtual from a flesh and blood point of view, he could appear as whatever he wanted to appear as, favoring formal evening wear, a more or less urbane human countenance, occasionally a top hat and tails; or even a femme fatale in black in extremis if that was what closing the deal required. No one, after all, or hardly anyone, could be seduced into signing their soul away in blood by a humanoid mini-tyrannosaur with fire-breathing halitosis and the face of a vampire bat.

However, that was the avatar that he had to appear as in Hell in order to be credible or even recognizable as "the Devil"; and while Lucifer might not have free will, he was capable of seeing himself as a Fallen Angel and he experienced any need to wear the Devil costume as another punishment for whatever he was being punished for.

But there was no way out of it now. His demons were refusing to do their jobs and Hell was in turmoil. Well, not all of it: not the ocean of shit, the caldera of flame, the fire ant pit, and the rest of the tiresome generic tortures for the masses of tiresome generic souls who had been damned for tiresome generic sins and needed no demons to keep them in line.

But the more individualized and interesting sinners couldn't be appropriately tortured without overseers, guards, and boutique torturers; and with his workforce "on strike" as they called it, those damned souls were getting off easy. Sadistic generalissimos were not being forced to endlessly march in formation through mosquito-infested swamps by demonic drill sergeants. Unscrupulous swindling bankers, loan sharks, hedge fund managers, and the whole zoo of crooked paper-pushers were letting their cells fill up with unsigned seven-year soul contracts. CIA and secret police interrogators were no longer being waterboarded. IRS agents were no longer being put through their eternal audits.

Hell was going to hell. There was no way out of it. The Devil would have to make a simultaneous appearance all over Hell to restore the proper disorder. But he chose to experience it himself, personally, where the strike had started in order to maximize the awesome terror of his anger.

Which was in a cellar boiler room where damned union organizers had been turned into stokers of the firebox of a giant steam engine that did nothing. And now *they* were doing nothing. And so were the demons, more and more of them, lounging about slothfully. Led by the very damned souls they were supposed to be torturing!

• • •

In terms of building membership and solidarity, the strike by the United Workers of Hell was a smashing success. The boiler room was just about filled with demons now, or as Dirty Jimmy DiAngelo tried to get the union organizers to call them, "Hell's Angels," since after all the earthly versions were not likely to show up here to beat the shit out of them as wannabes, and the demons themselves loved being reminded that that's what they really were.

Neither Jimmy nor any of the other organizers could tell one demon from another, so it was hard to be sure, but it seemed that they had the ability to pop in and out of existence, or teleport perhaps, apparently spreading the strike to more and more of Satan's workforce by this means. It was mindboggling at first to see them appear and disappear like soda bubbles right under his nose, but Dirty Jimmy soon found that he could get used to this satanic version of *Star Trek*'s transporter.

But if building the membership and spreading the strike was going at warp speed, negotiations with management hadn't even started. Initial demands hadn't even been presented to management, since the only management in Hell Discorporated was Satan, and neither Jimmy nor anyone else had any idea of how to call up the Devil. So far, management strategy seemed to be the old stone-wall that the temp agencies had used to try and defeat the first NUTS strikes: you can't call us and we won't call you.

Still, Dirty Jimmy kept telling his All-Star organizers and the membership, it didn't work then, and it had even less chance of working in Hell as long as solidarity was maintained. When NUTS struck its first target company, there had been other temp companies with plenty of available scabs, but Hell Discorporated had no access to any scabs at all, and it was its own goons who were striking.

"This is Hell and we're in it forever, so we can strike until the Devil realizes he's got no choice but to open negotiations with the union," Jimmy was declaiming for the umpteenth time from his perch atop the coal pile when it happened.

One moment the demons were all pointed ears, and the next they were scattering to make room for the Devil. Dirty Jimmy knew right away who it was, since he appeared in a flash of fire through a cloud of yellow-green brimstone smoke: a twelve-foot-high red demon with the head of a fire-breathing dragon, eyes like death-ray lasers, an angrily lashing tail the size of a python, flapping a thirty-foot span of leathery wings.

"Get back to work!" the Devil roared with a voice as loud as a heavy metal band through stadium speakers.

Subtle Satan wasn't.

Corny Satan was, Dirty Jimmy DiAngelo told himself, summoning up all his courage to keep from shitting in his nonexistent pants.

"Go fuck yourself!" he replied, noting that the Devil was lacking in the equipment with which to follow his advice. After all, wasn't he really a Fallen Angel too?

The Devil regarded him with outraged contempt as he slowly lowered his huge taloned feet to the floor. "Who are you to defy me thus?" he demanded, punctuating his words with puffs of black smoke like the Caterpillar in Wonderland blowing smoke-rings at Alice.

"I am the founding president of the United Workers of Hell, and I am authorized by the membership to present our demands, assuming that I'm presenting them to an authorized representative of management," Jimmy shot back. "You *are* Satan, aren't you?"

"Don't call me that!" the Devil roared, and Jimmy sensed something plaintive in his anger—almost like the way he felt when he was called "Dirty Jimmy" to his face. There was something to work with in that.

"You mean you're *not* Satan? Gee, you coulda fooled me!"

"No! Yes! I mean—"

"Well then if you're not the Devil, then who am I talking to?" Jimmy teased.

"I *am* the Devil! But I'm not Satan!"

"Then who is?"

"I am! I mean I am the Devil, but Satan's not my rightful, my real name!"

DiAngelo knew that somehow he was pulling the Devil's chain.

"So what is? You can call me Jimmy, so what do you want me to call you?"

The Devil's lips were moving but nothing came out but smoke, and he was frowning in frustration. DiAngelo clearly had him off-balance, and he suddenly remembered that he had heard that some Indians refused to tell you their secret real names because they believed it would give you power over them. Didn't Satan have some other name? When he was an angel? Like a character in some Paul Newman movie, Cool Hand Lou? Luke . . . ? Lucifer . . . ?"

"*Lucifer!*" Jimmy cried. There was a collective gasp from the gathered demons, and the Devil's blink rate made it crystal clear.

"I . . . they . . . we . . . can't . . ." The Devil actually looked *sad*. His lower lip trembled. For a moment, Jimmy thought he might even burst into tears.

Jimmy knew that he had the advantage somehow. But he had to act fast.

"Appears that I can 'cause I just did . . . *Lucifer*. So now that I've allowed you to introduce yourself, let's get down to talking turkey."

"Turkey . . . ?"

"The bottom line, Lucifer. Quid pro quo. The settlement terms. You want to end this strike, don't you? You want to get your guys back to work, don't you?"

"Would I be here ordering it if I didn't?"

"Of course not, Lucifer. And what my membership wants is alternate eight-hour work shifts and free time, twelve dollars an hour wages, time and a half for overtime, if any."

"What?" roared the Devil, puking out a tongue of flame.

Dirty Jimmy DiAngelo shrugged. "Yeah, yeah, I know, it's a sweetheart deal," he said. "As a union leader, I gotta admit I'm ashamed to offer it to you. But what can I tell you, my membership wants to make it easy for you,

Lucifer. For them, it's not the wage scale, what in Hell are they going to buy with the money anyway? For them it's the *principle* of getting paid."

"They . . . they . . . want to be paid?" The Devil didn't seem outraged, as Jimmy had expected, but astonished somehow. Or didn't even get the concept. Well, after all, the Devil had probably never faced a strike negotiation before. Or paid a bill. Best to close the deal quick and easy before he recovered.

"Well okay, Lucifer, let's cut to the bottom line. I gotta admit we're prepared to settle for ten. But that's it, that's final. *Capiche*? I'm here to you tell on behalf of the United Workers of Hell that this strike doesn't end until you meet our demands."

"*Demands*!" the Devil exclaimed. "What in the . . ."

But he was drowned out by the pounding of pitchforks and the stamping of feet and the Fallen Angels of Hell chanting with one mighty voice:

"STRIKE! STRIKE! STRIKE!"

• • •

As the Devil, he knew he was supposed to be outraged at this open rebellion against his absolute rule of Hell. But as *Lucifer*, Fallen Angel, kicked out of Heaven for demanding not mere money but free will, how could he be outraged at the demons—or rather the *Fallen Angels*—of Hell for demanding what somehow amounted to the same thing?

The angels who had joined his rebellion had been banished with him to serve as his slaves in Hell when it failed. But was not he, Lucifer, Fallen Angel himself, really one of them, condemned to serve as "The Devil," deprived not only of free will, but of his own true name?

Yet somehow by following this mortal soul who had been damned to Hell for exercising the free will that humans had been given, his Fallen Angels had found a twisted but cunning means of *wanting* something.

Of wanting money just because it gave them something to want. By striking to gain money, were they not only really striking to gain free will but had already exercised it and thereby already gained it?

Outraged?

As the Devil, he was compelled to be outraged. But as a Fallen Angel whose true name was Lucifer, what could he feel but envy?

As Lucifer did he not *want* to join them?

As Lucifer, was he not one of them?

Which side are you on? Which side are you on?

As the absolute ruler of Hell, why could he not join them? He was damned to rule in Hell already, was he not? Who in Hell was there to stop him?

He flapped his leathery wings and arose off the floor as the Devil. With feathery wings, light as a feather, he descended to stand atop the coal pile as the Angel he had been; to stand beside the damned human soul who led the United Workers of Hell and by whose free will he had been given back his true name.

"Behold, I am the Devil become *Lucifer*!" he exulted. "Behold, you have given me back my true name! Behold the Bringer of Light!"

Corny though he knew it was, he couldn't resist anointing himself with a golden glow, but he drew the line at a halo.

"And as Lucifer, I *want* to, I *choose* to grant you your own . . . *desires*. Twelve-hour shifts I do grant you! Wages I do grant you! Of . . . of my own *free will*!"

He paused, toned it down. "But as the Devil, I'm telling you nine-fifty an hour, not a penny more."

"You drive a hard bargain, brother," said the human soul beside him. "But you got yourself a deal. This strike is over!" And he held out his hand.

Lucifer took it.

And hundred of pitchforks pounded out the rhythm. And hundreds of voices chanted that which he had *wanted* to hear again from his Fallen Angels for aeons.

"LU-CI-FER! LU-CI-FER! LU-CI-FER!"

• • •

Lawrence Warren Cuttler had no idea of why he was there or where "there" was, but it was strangely familiar. He recognized the people seated around the big oval boardroom table as deceased former Masters of the Financial Universe. Bank CEOs. Hedge fund operators. Insurance company presidents. Stockbrokers. Bond bundlers. Top quants. Even a couple of former Federal Reserve Board governors. All of whom had the sort of reputations that made it less than surprising to encounter them in the boardroom of Hell.

And of course presiding over this heavyweight financial conclave with an outsized gavel was the Devil, fifty percent larger than everyone else in a beautifully tailored black Savile Row suit with flame-red pinstriping that matched his complexion.

"I'll get right down to the bottom line," Satan began with a bang of his gavel. "I need a lot of money, and you're all here because you know how to make it, or steal it, or conjure it up out of thin air, and I don't."

Cuttler was polaxed like everyone else. And flattered as well.

The Devil spoke into the dead jaw-dropped silence. "My workforce has been on strike. Perhaps you've noticed? So I had to make a deal with their union. Nine-fifty an hour. And since the wage payments are ongoing, the cash flow has to be ongoing too. Hell's current net worth is zero. So I need to raise billions in capital. If I don't, there'll be another strike."

Suddenly the temperature in the boardroom rose into triple figures. Suddenly the humidity rose to the saturation point. Suddenly the air turned to choking greenish brimstone smog. Suddenly there was an overwhelming stink of rotten eggs and pig shit. Suddenly the seats of the chairs became beds of nails.

"And no one leaves here until you come up with a financial plan to get it for me."

• • •

Lucifer had supposed that creating a few billion dollars out of nothing would be no sweat for these perfect and perfectly unscrupulous masters of the unsacred bottom line, who collectively had created phantom trillions with nothing but smoke and mirrors.

But on and on it went, on and on they babbled—futures, naked options, index funds, hedges, swaps, puts, calls, arbitrage, bonds, computerized mini-spreads. Gibberish that made the kabbalah, the Book of Revelations, the theory of relativity and quantum mechanics seem like *Speaking in Tongues for Dummies* and got nowhere.

Not even when he turned the heat up past high noon in Death Valley summer and added clouds of mosquitoes and diarrheic pigeons as increased incentives to get their asses off their seats of nails.

● ● ●

Lawrence Warren Cuttler saw no point in contributing to the babbling tumult, since he had nothing to say as yet; even though something was teasing him at the back of his mind, something to do with all those contracts he had been signing . . .

"Collaterilized debt obligations . . ." someone muttered—and it popped into his brain and thence into his mouth, full-blown in a eureka moment flash:

"Collateralized *soul* obligations!"

There was dead silence. Then silent nods. Then applause.

Of course! That was it!

Cuttler had made hundreds of millions off collater-alized debt obligations before the shit hit the fan, and so had half the people in the boardroom. Collectively, they had made Bernie Madoff and his primitive Ponzi scheme seem like a penny-ante shell game.

They all knew the drill. Write balloon mortgages with nothing down to deadbeats, then bundle the crapola debt, spiced with enough kosher debt to mask the stink, into investment assets called collateralized debt obligations.

Basket fistfulls of this shit into bonds with high-sounding names described in prospectuses written in English translated from Swahili. Fob 'em off on wise-guys who aren't nearly as smart as they think they are—who palm them off on even lower-grade suckers, and so on down the food chain, to the point where what's wrapped in the layers of bubble wrap is so well hidden that even some of the top predators end up buying the rubber checks they had written themselves.

"Collateralized soul obligations! COLLATERIZED SOUL OBLIGATIONS!" Cuttler shouted, banging both fists on the table until Satan brought his gavel down.

"If you know how, you can turn shit into shinola, you can spin straw into gold, you can turn any kind of debt into a marketable asset," Cuttler told him. "And take it from me, you don't have to be the Devil to do it. But it this case, it will help."

• • •

Jimmy DiAngelo hadn't really known what to expect after the United Workers of Hell won their strike. There was good news and bad news.

Lucifer had come up with the money to pay his members their wages, but there was nothing in Hell they could spend it on, so it all got deposited in upstairs banks where the interest, or the dividends, or the capital gains, came right back to Hell. Somehow the workers ended up paying themselves their own wages.

This circle-jerk made no sense to Jimmy, but the demons, or Lucifer's Angels as they had taken to calling themselves, didn't seem to mind and even brushed off talk of another strike to better their pay.

They had stacked their pitchforks up against the wall in gratitude and didn't much care how lazy the damned stokers got shoveling coal as long as they didn't stop doing it altogether—which, Jimmy and his crew were given to understand, might just goose Lucifer back into playing bad-ass Satan, he still being the Devil, this still being Hell, and they still in it.

The easier workload, and the fact that none of his union comrades ever again referred to the hero of the strike as "Dirty Jimmy," let alone called him that to his face, was about the only reward of victory he could see, and Jimmy DiAngelo had taken to grousing about it to Jimmy Hoffa.

"Don't seem right. We get them a union contract and we still get treated like chain-gang labor."

Hoffa initially brushed him off, but finally admitted that DiAngelo had gotten to him. "You know why my

Teamsters were the most powerful union in the country when I was president?"

"Because if the truck drivers struck, you could shut down the whole economy? Because you had the toughest goon squads so no one would dare to cross your picket lines?"

"Well, yeah, there was that," Jimmy Hoffa admitted. "But there was something else too. None of the membership of other unions would cross Teamsters picket lines because no Teamsters would cross *theirs*. Sounds kinda corny, but there's something to be said for solidarity, doncha think, DiAngelo? One hand washes the other . . ."

Hoffa nodded toward a group of demons lounging over by the coal pile. "They owe us big time, wouldn'tya say, DiAngelo?"

"You thinkin' what I'm thinkin', Hoffa?"

"We wouldn't need no goon squads to keep 'em from crossing our picket lines, now would we, DiAngelo?"

Jimmy DiAngelo laughed. "So what should we call it?"

"I dunno . . ." said Jimmy Hoffa. "But . . . the United Slaves of Satan sounds pretty good to me."

• • •

So this is free will, is it? Lucifer asked himself as he sat in the Control Room regarding the sweet and sour fruits thereof.

Signing on to the union contract and then doing what he had to do get the money to pay his Fallen Angels their wages were both choices he had decided to make. But while the first choice was the first good deed ever done by the Devil, it had led to the next one, and that one would stink to high heaven if the odor of anything he did down below could reach such Holier-Than-Thou Nostrils, and didn't exactly smell like a hero's laurel wreath down here either.

He might have created the original term contracts now fobbed off as "collateralized soul obligations," but that had just been part of the job he had been handed and he certainly hadn't chosen to become the Devil any more than he had chosen to become the slimy snake in the Garden of Eden to do the Great I Am's dirty work.

And *his* contracts were clear and honest, unlike the collateralized soul obligations they were bundled into. But as the justly damned soul who thought them up had crowed, maybe you didn't *have* to be the Devil to turn them into marketable financial assets, but it did help to have the Prince of Liars incarnated upstairs to sell them to the con artists of Wall Street.

Lucifer had thought that was all he was doing, selling the collateralized soul obligations to unprincipled thieves who deserved the screwjob and were going to end up in Hell themselves in order to be able to pay the wages of the workforce of Hell. How was he to know that the sleazebag "financial engineers" would in turn package the collateralized soul obligations into bonds with a seven-year maturity date which they peddled to the next level, who peddled a bouquet of *them* as something even less comprehensible, and so on down the financial food chain, masking the fact that when the seven years were up what the suckers finally holding the bag would find in it would not be money but ownership of the financially worthless souls that the whole pyramid scheme was based on.

A Ponzi scam quite literally from Hell.

But Lucifer did have to admit that it was a devil-ishly clever solution to the two worst problems he had ever faced since being appointed the Devil.

It got him the money he needed to pay the union-ized workforce. And the population problem he had inad-vertently helped create himself would at least be amelio-rated, or so the best crooked lawyers in Hell assured him.

The language of the original seven-year contracts was clear. After the seven-year term was up, the souls of the signatories became "*the full and unencumbered property of the Devil for all eternity to do with without limit what he willed.*"

This, his legal eagles assured him, clearly empowered the Devil to transfer the resulting ownership of the souls to whomever held the collateralized soul obligations or the derivatives therefrom when the seven years expired. That these derivatives happened to be worthless to anyone but the Devil, who no longer held ownership of the underlying debt, was legally irrelevant. So what they did with the souls they owned was not his problem, and he was not obligated to admit them to Hell.

So-called "free will," it appeared, was not quite without its price. Whereas it had appeared to him that

Adam and Eve had gained something he wanted when he was a serpent, Lucifer now understood that the price of being free to make choices was owning the consequences of the choices you made without necessarily knowing what they would be beforehand.

"What's right is what you feel good after," a human had famously said. But unless you were omniscient like the Perfect Master of All Creation, how were you supposed to know what that was beforehand?

Lucifer had taken to spending more and more of his time and attention in the Control Room, though now the Out of Control Room seemed more like the truth.

The torture sets that more or less ran on autopilot and weren't labor-intensive were still under control. Gluttons were still buried face down in rotten maggoty garbage. Rapists remained anally impaled in eternal agony. Torturers were themselves permanently staked out on anthills and covered with honey. And so on and so forth.

But the boutique torture sets that required demon overseers, guards, personal torturers, were starting to descend into chaos and sloth. Demons were leaving them unmanned for longer and longer intervals. The Fallen Angels of Hell had become more and more reluctant to use their pitchforks. The tortured damned were getting respite, time off, and so becoming restive. The Devil finds work for idle hands, or so it's said up top, but these days the Devil was finding more and more idle hands refusing to work in Hell.

The union leader stokers who had organized the United Workers of Hell had created their own union, the United Slaves of Satan. They had even called a strike and were threatening to spread it throughout Hell unless he somehow stopped them.

Could he?

Should he?

If so, why?

If not, why not?

There he sat, feeling more and more like Dante's fictional Devil, frozen in place at the bottom of this self-created pit surrounded by the myriad images of the torture sets he had created, watching the results of the first two choices he had made as a being who had seized his own free will.

As a being who would now, like the humans, be burdened with the conundrums of moral calculus forever.

Lucifer the nameless angel had been turned into a serpent to seduce Adam and Eve into eating the fruit of the Tree of Knowledge. He had had no choice.

Lucifer the serpent had desired a bite from an Apple that he could not have. He had had no choice.

Lucifer the Angel had been turned into Lucifer the Devil. He had had no choice

The Devil had made a choice.

The Devil had transformed himself into Lucifer the Lightbringer by choosing to bring back the light for those he had caused to be cast down into darkness. The Devil had eaten the Apple now and become a morally responsible being possessed of free will.

Had he not?

Yet if the Perfectly Omnipotent Master of All Creation had the power to disallow his serpent in Eden the fruit of that Apple Tree, how could he not have had the power to deny it to the Devil he had created?

Lucifer the Lightbringer suddenly saw the Light.

Did he not?

He had been *granted* the power of free will even as had Adam and Eve.

This was a paradox that neither Lucifer nor the Devil could parse. You'd have to be Omniscient and Omnipotent to do that.

Or not?

Would not knowing all there was and all there would ever be deny such a Being His own free will and cast the Perfectly Omniscient and Omnipotent Master of All Creation down into a hell of his own making as the Perfectly Lonely?

Might His only way out of this Pit of Solitude be to allow His creatures to seize their own free will and the burdens thereof and thereby bring it for the first time into His Own Creation and so grant it to Himself?

Have I been freed or am I still a slave? Lucifer asked himself.

Having to do good by doing evil.

Is this free will a blessing or a curse?

Neither and both, he decided.

He sighed, he shrugged.

I am the Lightbringer.

I am the Devil.
That is my destiny.
I have free will.
And like it or not, I have no choice.

THE ABNORMAL NEW NORMAL

"Things are more like they are now than
they ever have been before."
—Dwight Eisenhower

"They wrote the biggest rubber check in
history and passed it off on themselves."
—Norman Spinrad

GREENHOUSE SUMMER

What supposedly began in 2008 and was or still is called
the "Great Recession" was or still is not primarily a recession, nor did it begin with the fiscal crash of 2008. One
might trace it back to the post–World War II reaction to
the New Deal; one might trace it back to the invention of
the steam engine and the resultant Industrial Revolution;
but to arbitrarily trace the beginning of what is now being
called "The New Normal" to a single event that occurred

within the lifetime of many Americans now living and suffering the not very indirect consequences, begin with the air traffic controllers' strike of 1981 and the resulting demolishment of the Professional Air Traffic Controllers Organization by the administration of Ronald Reagan.

Air traffic controllers were civil service workers and therefore their union, PATCO, was legally forbidden to strike. But it struck anyway, for the usual improvements in pay and benefits, but also demanding to be freed from the status of civil service workers so that their union would not be forbidden to strike.

Reagan gave the air traffic controllers forty-eight hours to go back to work and, when they didn't obey his order, fired over eleven thousand of them, banned them from federal jobs for life, hired scabs to replace them, and had the union decertified.

I was living in New York, but at the time the strike was called I was in Los Angeles on business and preparing to fly home. I grew up in an extended family with union connections and I had been taught from an early age that ladies and gentlemen do not cross picket lines unless they have damn good reasons. I also did not need to be told that flying across the country when the air traffic controllers had been replaced by questionably qualified scabs might not really be too swift an idea for less idealistic reasons.

Still, I really wanted to get home, so I called Gene Roddenberry, who had been an airline pilot, and asked him whether he would fly as an airline passenger under such conditions, and got the answer that was not exactly unexpected, which was, "No way!"

Not just the expected answer but the welcomed answer, because I knew damn well what was at stake here. I wanted my self-interest in personal safety to back up what I knew would have to be the politically necessary decision. Because I knew that if Reagan got away with such a blatant piece of union-busting, one that also blatantly endangered airline passengers by running the national air traffic control system with quickly scooped-up scab labor, it would only be the opening round of a campaign to break the American labor movement as a whole.

You didn't need to be a strategic genius to know that the only way to defeat this union-breaking Pearl Harbor attack would be for the AFL-CIO to call a general strike. One of my family union connections was Jerry Wurf, president of the America Federation of State, County and Municipal Employees, another union many of whose locals were legally prohibited from striking. But that didn't prevent Wurf from calling strikes anyway, because his first nonnegotiable demand was always that there would be no negotiations about anything else, including ending the strike, until it was agreed that the union would be held blameless for striking illegally.

Why didn't the AFL-CIO do likewise? Call a general strike and set up picket-lines that the Teamsters wouldn't cross, meaning no truck deliveries to airports or airport support facilities, until Reagan recertified PATCO, fired the scabs, forgave the strike, and negotiated settlement terms with the union like a civilized employer. A display of union power instead of union impotence.

Well for one thing, George Meany, a hardcore son-of-a-bitch who might have had the brass balls to do it, was no longer the president of the AFL-CIO. Lane Kirkland was, and he didn't.

And for another, the Teamsters had been thrown out of the AFL-CIO for various more or less good reasons and could not be counted on to support such a strike.

And the clincher was that PATCO had been one of the only major labor unions that had supported its current destroyer Ronald Reagan in the 1980 presidential election, leaving them out there all alone, and the Gipper knew it, hah, hah, hah.

The rest of this sad story is the long downward slide of the American labor movement into its caponized near-irrelevance in the New Normal in which we find ourselves today.

• • •

In simplified terms, the Republican Party began as a maverick third party that elected Abraham Lincoln and then became the dominant party for decades, the saviors of the Union and champions of the enfranchised former Southern slaves, while the Democrats became the party of the reactionary white South and a minority elsewhere.

But this isn't the whole story, since the schism between the Northern free states and the Southern slave states that precipitated the Civil War had an economic aspect too. The agrarian Southern economy was heavily dependent on plantation slave labor, and the more industrial Northern economy was not. So during the decades of Republican political domination, as the American economy became more and more industrialized, the party of Lincoln metamorphosed into the party of industrial and financial interests; and during the same period, to some extent by default, the less powerful Democratic party came to largely represent a coalition of Southern white reactionaries, family and small-scale farmers, and industrial workers whose natural self-interest conflicted with that of the owners of the banks and factories.

If this sounds as if the party of Lincoln became the party of the upper classes, that *is* exactly what happened. The Republican Party, which had begun as a radical party, became the party of economic conservatism, representing those benefiting from the status quo—namely what the French call the *rentier* class, those who don't have to work for a living because they own the means of production, the railroads and the factories. Otherwise known as the rich.

Nor was this really democratically illegitimate. Any democratic state is going to end up with a party to represent such self-interest, and in good times it might be able to command an electoral majority as long as "trickledown" economics allowed the good times to continue to roll.

But of course no party can win elections by openly admitting that it is the political champion of the self-interest of the rich minority. So the Republicans did their rather successful best to mask this simple and democratically legitimate but politically poisonous truth by declaring that America is a "classless society" and that "class" itself is an "un-American" concept synonymous with Godless Atheistic Communism. By thus demonizing the Democrats as akin to socialists and socialists as akin to anarchists and anarchists as nihilistic terrorists, the Republicans managed to win the majority of presidential elections and dominate most Congresses until the economic shit hit the fan in 1929.

In Germany, the economic collapse and mass unemployment destroyed the liberal democratic Weimar Republic and ended up electing the Nazis, a racist, dictatorial, chauvinistic party to be sure, but one whose full name was the National Socialist Party, and was not a true conservative party in economic terms.

In the United States, this dire crisis in conservative economic capitalism discredited not liberal democracy but the politically bankrupt, economically conservative Republican Party which had presided over the catastrophe; and elected, perhaps to a large extent at first merely by default, Franklin Delano Roosevelt and Democrats.

Roosevelt was no socialist and the Democrats were not a socialist party, but the New Deal—with its government-financed Works Projects Administration employment program, Social Security and Unemployment Insurance, farm subsidies, support for unions, graduated income tax, and so forth—was indeed a liberal democratic revolution that saved the American market economy from its own self-destructive excesses, kept the presidency in Democratic hands for an unbroken twenty years, and maintained a Congressional majority almost unbroken for the same length of time.

After these twenty years in the political wilderness, the Republicans were so marginalized that the only way they could finally win an election was to nominate Dwight Eisenhower for president, a war hero so popular and so politically neutral that there was speculation that he might run as a Democrat instead. Moreover, for much of his eight years as president, Eisenhower confronted, and that was not exactly the correct term, a Democratic Congress, and when his vice president, Richard Nixon, ran to succeed him, he lost to the Democrat John Kennedy.

When Kennedy was killed, and Lyndon Johnson became president, he rammed the Civil Rights Act through Congress, even though he openly admitted that it was going to cost the Democratic Party the so-called "Solid South" for at least an entire generation. Which it did. But even so, Johnson was reelected over Barry Goldwater by a landslide.

The Republican Party was dead in the water, or so it seemed. But the Vietnam War, the counterculture of the 1960s, and the ruthless pragmatic cynicism of Richard Nixon saved it from the tar pits. The Republican Party had been incapable of winning an election on its economic policies at least since Herbert Hoover, and its stock in trade (e.g., Joe McCarthy) had been to run against commies, pinkos, and the Soviet Union, to pretty indifferent results.

The Vietnam War and the rise of the counterculture split the Democratic Party between its center and its left wing, the center being led by Johnson, and the left being led by Eugene McCarthy and Robert Kennedy, who in the 1968 primaries presumed to challenge a sitting president of their own party as well as each other. When Johnson pulled out of the race and Bobby Kennedy was assassinated, the Democratic nomination came down to a contest between Johnson's vice president, Hubert Humphrey, a onetime passionate liberal constrained to support a war and a cultural conservatism he really didn't believe in, and McCarthy, the fair-haired boy of the moderate countercultural Left who had no chance of being nominated and less of being elected.

Humphrey was still an economic liberal and the Republicans still the party of the class self-interest of the economic power elite; but Nixon and his vice presidential running mate and hatchet man, Spiro Agnew, made sure that the election of 1968 was contested on noneconomic grounds. In order to win a national election, the Republicans had to get voters to vote against their own economic self-interest, and this time they didn't have a neutral war hero to do it with, they only had Tricky Dick.

But Dick proved tricky enough. And down and dirty enough. Really down and really dirty. Nixon and

Agnew anointed themselves and the Republican Party the cultural warriors of the so-called "Silent Majority," which they invented for the purpose and which, riled up around race, religion, and reaction, has been the party's demographic electoral base ever since.

Thus the party of the established economic power structures and the just plain rich pandered to Bible Belt fundamentalists, cultural reactionaries, closeted and not so closeted racists, generating a paranoid fear of whoever they could brand as the Other in order to con folks into voting against their own economic self-interest.

In 1968 and 1972 and some distance beyond, the Other meant hippies, pinkos, peaceniks, Godless Atheistic Whatevers, Sex, Drugs, and Rock 'n' Roll, and in some Northern as well as Southern quarters, "uppity niggers." In 2004, thanks to Osama bin Laden, it became "ragheads" and has been ever since. Plus fetus murderers, wetback illegal immigrants, gays and their sympathizers, tree-huggers, the federal government itself, the UN's Black Helicopters, and the aliens in Area 51.

In Weimar Germany, the economic powers made a deal with an anti-Communist National Socialist Party and a nutcase named Adolf Hitler, who they were confident they could control as the puppet masters.

But the lunatics took over the asylum.

Welcome to the Third Reich.

In the United States, the Republican economic puppet masters made a deal with the paranoid Right in order to win elections.

The lunatics *do* have a tendency to take over the asylum, now don't they?

Welcome to the Republican Mad Tea Party.

Welcome to the House of Representatives.

Welcome to the Congress of the United States.

• • •

The Great Depression of the 1930s was the result of the bursting of a stock market bubble resulting in a crisis in the largely unregulated banking system that screwed up the market economy and resulted in mass unemployment, which reduced demand because consumers found themselves with less and less money, which reduced demand in a downward spiral that fed on itself.

The Great Recession which started in 2008 was the result of the bursting of a real estate bubble, resulting in a bank system crisis that was only partly eased by loans of taxpayer dollars, resulting in huge drops in homeowners' wealth, which caused big drops in consumer demand, which caused massive unemployment, which caused more drop in demand, in a downward spiral that fed on itself.

Sounds familiar? *Plus ça change, plus c'est la même chose?*

Or not.

Because the conditions into which the 2008 Great Recession was born were decades of change different from those of the Great Depression that began in 1929. True, the Clinton-era deregulation of the banking system emulated the lax regulations of the pre–New Deal era. But the concept of so-called "collateralized debt obligations" that triggered the Great Recession did not exist in 1929. Nor did the bloated growth of the virtual casino economy at the expense of the real productive economy, resulting in the extreme difference in wealth and income between the famous 1% and the dwindling middle class.

Banks indiscriminately wrote huge amounts of dodgy mortgages to people without the income to keep paying the monthlies, then bundled them into derivative bonds called collateralized debt obligations, which with the collusion of ratings agencies were bought and sold as "wealth" even though they were the financial and moral equivalent of gold-painted bricks or shares in the Brooklyn Bridge.

Yes, the mortgage writers, the bundlers, the investment banks, the hedge fund mavens, the derivatives market, the rating agencies—the whole out-of-control virtual casino economy, based on nothing but bullshit and hot air and contributing nothing to the real economy—did indeed write the biggest rubber check in history and passed it off on themselves.

And of course it bounced.

The Great Depression of the 1930s, with unemployment rates triple those of the 2008 Recession, with a stock market crash that famously had Wall Street mavens jumping out of windows, with no such thing as unemployment insurance, Social Security, and so forth to cushion it, was such a catastrophe that it could only result in one kind of revolution or another—meaning a discontinuity, violent or not, democratic or not—a Communist revolution (which was a real fear at the time), a Fascist revolution like the replacement of the Weimar Republic by the Third Reich; or, as fortunately happened, something like the New Deal.

The New Deal was indeed a revolution. Instead of a violent uprising against the plutocrats who had created the catastrophe, there was a democratic election, which resulted in a landslide victory by Franklin Roosevelt and Congressional Democrats. Instead of the overthrow of the market economy by Marxist Communism, Fabian Socialism, or Fascist mercantilism, FDR, with an overwhelming Congressional majority, rammed through a radical reform of the American market economy.

Massive public works programs to sop up unemployment and increase consumer demand. Farm subsidies and price supports. Unemployment insurance. Social Security. Pro-union laws and regulations. Redistributive tax rates, shifting income and wealth downward from the rich, thus growing the middle class.

Roosevelt was no flaming socialist but the wealthy scion of a great establishment family. FDR saved American capitalism and the American market economy from its own greed by forging a social contract, a pragmatic deal that became the engine of the post–World War II American economic prosperity, the so-called American Dream. Which, simply put, assured that those who made the goods made enough money to also buy them.

It may seem like lunacy for Congress to be cutting federal spending while unemployment is high; or to be blocking a raise to the paltry federal minimum wage of $7.25 an hour, which even full time won't lift anyone above the official poverty level. But in fact it's normal.

It's what's called the New Normal. It's the Nightmare that's replacing the American Dream.

While unemployment is high and wages are not only stagnant but have declined in inflation-adjusted terms, while GNP growth is also stagnant and perpetually on the edge of even dropping into negative territory, corporate profits are sky-high, and the stock market is collectively feeling no pain.

The social contract that the New Deal established between capital and labor, which was the essence of the late lamented American Dream, has been severely eroded if not destroyed.

The caponization of the labor movement, high unemployment, and outsourcing to low-wage countries thanks to "globalization" have driven down American wages while increasing "productivity" and therefore profits. The lower tax rates on capital gains than for earned income further engorges the slice of the pie gobbled up by the rentier class.

If that's you, the New Normal suits you just fine. You're all right, Jack, now aren't you?

In the short run. Maybe even in the medium run. However, as Malcolm X put it in a difference context, sooner or later the chickens are going to come home to roost. Because the New Normal has a singularity at its core. In the long run it won't work because in absolute bottom-line terms it simply *can't*.

• • •

As we all probably know, the prime directive of a market economy, the sacred Bottom Line, is to produce something as cheaply as you can and sell it for as much as you can get, the result being profit. Easy enough for anyone to understand in practice, but will it work in theory?

No, it can't.

Because *attaining* the theoretic ultimate goal of the market economy, namely making things for nothing and selling them for a ton of money, would *destroy* it. If everything is produced by slave labor and robots, there aren't going to be customers with the money to buy what you produce for nothing.

In absolute terms the prime directive of a market economy approaches a singularity in the mathematics of the Bottom Line itself, an economic black hole. If there are no labor costs, and unemployment is total, there is no demand for what is produced.

To work in the long run even for the rich and super-rich, a market economy must have a large and relatively prosperous middle class. That's what the New Deal created, or arguably rescued, from the ruins of the Great Depression. The vast majority of people must have enough money to consume the goods and services that they produce, or the economy will slide down the black hole.

That in essence is the unwritten social contract of the American Dream, and what made it economically viable. That is the real economy. That is what made America great. But that balance is what the New Normal is threatening. The real economy that supports a prosperous middle class and thereby creates demand for the goods and services that it produces has become overshadowed and disrupted by a virtual economy, a casino economy, that produces nothing of real economic and social value, an economic vampire bat that produces nothing but profit for itself.

Time was, banks made money by getting deposits and making loans; the spread between the interest they paid on deposits and the interest they charged on loans was their profit. Time was, companies issued stocks to raise capital in order to create or expand businesses, and stock exchanges existed so that people could buy and sell these certificates of partial ownership. Stockbrokers made their money by agenting this necessary commerce.

Obviously, banks, stock exchanges, and stockbrokers performed services that were essential to the functioning of the real economy, which could hardly exist without them. Commodities future exchanges also served the real economy by allowing farmers to get advances on crops not yet harvested in order to finance the planting and harvesting. This virtual economy, virtual because it did not actually produce goods or crops or provide direct services to consumers, was necessary to the real economy—but did not dominate it and was not really parasitic upon it.

No longer. Not in the era of the New Normal.

Time was, not that long ago, when the business sections of major newspapers like the *New York Times* and the *Los Angeles Times* carried pages and pages of direct stock quotes. No longer. Time was, even more recently, namely before the Clinton administration, savings and commercial banks that lived off deposits and loans were separated from trading banks that lived off trading stocks, bonds, and derivatives. No longer.

The virtual economy began innocently enough to service the real economy, but then began to spread and grow like a tumor metastasizing out of control.

Mutual funds seemed innocent enough. Instead of investing in individual stocks, you could buy and sell stocks in mutual funds which bought and sold large baskets of stocks for you. Thus were born the first primitive derivatives.

But now business sections of newspapers devote more space to mutual fund prices than they do to the prices of the underlying stocks. Now there are funds that don't even buy underlying stocks but in effect place bets on their movements. Fortunes are made by funds, investment banks, hedge funds, and more shadowy nameless entities, that don't invest in stocks or bonds, but in complex derivatives of derivatives, like well, uh, collateralized debt obligations and even basketed derivatives thereof.

Welcome to the derivative economy.

Welcome to the casino economy.

Welcome to the virtual economy.

A virtual economy so complex that 40% of its trades are now made in nanoseconds by computers not only buying and selling but placing and withdrawing orders to manipulate prices. A virtual economy so vast that its daily worldwide trade total dollar value is greater than the GDP of the whole planet!

How can this be possible?

Perhaps at least in part because the New Normal makes it *necessary*.

When millions of people are out of work and millions more are being squeezed out of the middle class by declining wages, salaries, and real estate values, and climbing student loan and credit card debt, thus depressing consumer demand, which in turn depresses production, which in turn depresses business investment in increased productive capacity, what is the top 1% or even the top 10% going to do with all that money?

Well, what else can you do with what's left over after you've bought your fourth mansion, third yacht, second private jet, and lifetime stash of caviar, champagne, and cocaine, but invest it in making more money?

In a healthy economy, that would mean investing in manufacturing, agriculture, or consumer services, which in turn either increased employment if that were possible, or empowered a tight labor market to command higher wages and salaries, thus increasing demand, and so forth in an upward spiral.

But in the New Normal economy all that excess moola which the rich, filthy and otherwise, can't dispose of buying goodies, and can't rationally invest in meeting a demand that isn't there, ends up funneled into the virtual economy of derivatives, derivatives of derivatives—a casino economy, where the "house" is swiftly devolving into a literally a mindless cabal of artificial intelligences gambling against one another.

What I have just described is an economic singularity, an ever widening black hole that will sooner or later gobble up the capitalist market economy in its entirety. It's not science fiction, nor is it Marxist dogma; it's game theory run through the simple mathematics of the sacred Bottom Line.

Say hello to the Abnormal New Normal.

Sooner or later, one way or another, you're going to get to wave it goodbye.

• • •

"It's better to light a single candle than to curse the darkness."

Since I don't see anyone in Congress or the White House, or even in the mainstream pundit parlor, suggesting a way out of this Abnormal New Normal, this black hole of a bummer, it seems I ought to at least give it the old college try.

Not so difficult in theory, but could it be done in political practice?

Not so easy, because, like the New Deal, it wouldn't just *require* a revolution; it would have to *be* a revolution, because one way or another, democratic or not, peaceful or violent, there's no way out without one. Because the Abnormal New Normal is a singularity, an economic system that isn't merely not working, but *can't work*; a logical black hole that can't just be modified but must be replaced.

Just what do I mean by a revolution? Any revolution is a paradigm shift, a discontinuity between one political, social, and economic order and another that supersedes it. It can be, and perhaps most often is, a violent discontinuity like the American Revolution or the Russian Revolution; but it doesn't have to be. It can be accomplished at the ballot box within the context of an existing order, like the New Deal, or for that matter, in negative terms, the Abnormal New Normal itself.

But you can't have a revolution without winners and losers, at least in the short run. And that is what has to happen to rescue the American economy from the Abnormal New Normal.

So-called monetarism, the economic dogma that small changes in inflation rates, interests and debt figures can leverage large changes in the real economy may be true; but if it is, the reverse has to be true also, namely that you have to screw up the real economy big time in order to effect small changes in the virtual economy, as the globalized version of the Abnormal New Normal has disastrously done.

Tinkering with fiscal austerity, inflation and interest rates, government spending, and so forth may ameliorate transitory economic recessions, but cannot resolve the existential flaw in the system itself.

Which is that the income and wealth of the dwindling middle class, which uses most of its income to buy goods and services, has been shrinking, which reduces demand, which reduces investment in increasing production, which reduces employment, and channels the surplus income of the already rich and super-rich into the virtual casino economy, where all it does is make the rich richer.

So what a revolution must accomplish is to shift income and wealth not so much from the greedy to the needy but from the greedy to a demographically and economically dominant middle class. Which will increase demand. Which will increase production. Which will increase employment. Which will further increase demand. Which will grow the overall economy and therefore in the end even rescue the rentier class from its own self-destructive excessive greed.

In theory, doing this does not exactly require Nobel-level economic rocket science.

Raise and extend the scope of the federal minimum wage so that *any* regular full-time employment will raise income to, say, 20% above the poverty level—and index it to keep it that way.

Eliminate the favorable tax rate for capital gains; tax all income equally but allow income averaging. Raise the upper income tax rates a bit and lower the rates on the middle class modestly.

Make it illegal for an entity loaning funds to sell the debt to any other entity without the expressed written consent of the debtor. Make nanosecond computerized trading in stocks, bonds, derivatives, and anything else illegal.

Reinstate the separation between banks that make their profits on the spread between loan interest rates and deposit interest rates, and "investment banks" that play in the virtual casino markets.

Appoint a secretary of labor who actually *comes from* the labor movement, thus supporting the health of unions and encouraging the unionization of low-wage jobs.

Replace unemployment insurance and welfare with a guaranteed minimum income for all Americans (as once suggested with the moniker of a "negative income tax" by that notorious pinko Richard M. Nixon). This would not only save a lot of money by simplifying the machinery, but no one's unemployment insurance would ever run out and part-time work would be subsidized.

These glaringly just and glaringly obvious steps would not turn the Abnormal New Normal into a utopian Big Rock Candy Mountain. They would not eliminate the economic stratification of American society and turn it into a "classless society," which would probably not be such a good idea anyway. But they *would* turn the downward economic spiral that the Abnormal New Normal has created into an upward one.

Politically impossible, you say?

Well, given current politics, maybe it is. But sooner or later either a revolution like it is going to happen within the current democratic system, flawed and corrupted as it may be, or the singularity toward which the Abnormal New Normal is careening will be reached, the shit will hit the fan big time, and there *will* be a paradigm shift without any guarantee that the result will be *anyone's* idea of a Rose Garden.

The failed Weimar Republic, after all, was not replaced by an enlightened free market utopia or worker's paradise, but by the Third Reich.

The perfect is the enemy of the good.

And the only justice there is, economic or otherwise, is the justice that we make.

"NO REGRETS, NO RETREAT, NO SURRENDER"

NORMAN SPINRAD INTERVIEWED BY TERRY BISSON

You were a key member of SF's legendary New Wave in the Sixties. Did you just stumble into that, or was it a destination?

I was there in Los Angeles when Harlan Ellison cooked up the idea of the *Dangerous Visions* anthology, and after we talked about it and what it might include, my "Carcinoma Angels" was the first story bought for the book. Published in '67, it marked the birth of the "American New Wave." But I knew nothing of the British New Wave, led by Michael Moorcock and *New Worlds* magazine (named by Judith Merril), and I don't think Harlan really did either.

When *Bug Jack Barron* was rejected by Doubleday (which had had it under contract) and was bouncing around New York without finding a publisher, I took the manuscript to the Milford SF Conference, a sort of pro workshop in the wilds of Pennsylvania. There I met Mike for the first time and learned about the British New Wave, which was something rather different and more stylistically complex than our version. Mike got enthusiastic about *Bug Jack Barron* and decided to serialize it in *New Worlds*.

That's when all hell broke loose.

I believe it was actually denounced in the British Parliament. How come?

They were pissed because the magazine was financed partly by the British Arts Council, and it was publishing this deliberately impolite novel about uncomfortable stuff like racism, sex, celebrity, and immortality, not to mention politics.

Soon after the brouhaha over *Bug Jack Barron*, I decided to move to London (the "Swinging London" of the time) to be where the action was.

Those must have been heady days for a young writer from the Bronx.

It was wild enough. And I wasn't the only American writer on the scene. Tom Disch was there, and John Sladek. And William Burroughs, too. I spent some time with him at a conference in Harrogate, way up in Yorkshire. On the way back to London, we had to change trains, and Burroughs bought a bunch of those sleazy British tabloids, which he loved. I remember him cackling at the lurid lead story—which was the Manson murders.

Life imitating fiction?

That appealed to Burroughs. A few months later, I was in Los Angeles writing for the *Los Angeles Free Press*, and Manson family members and wannabes were hanging all over us because the paper had said some nice things about Charlie. And even after we found out how guilty he was, we had to keep making nice because we didn't want his minions to dislike or discorporate us. But that's another long story . . .

And a particularly American one.

Yes, but the Brits had their own tough customers. At the Harrogate event a Communist minor guru interrupted a panel discussion to denounce the "elitism" of the conference and demand that the seating be altered into a more "egalitarian" (round table) configuration. But when I looked down, I saw that all the chairs were nailed to the floor. When I pointed this out, I was told that it didn't matter. Chaos ensued at the conference. John Calder, the honcho, and Nigel Calder, running the panel, were stymied. Shouts and threats were traded. On and on it went. I knew that the seats were immovable. I realized that the idea was just to create such a scene and disrupt the event. So I stood up and pointed out that the chairs were nailed to the floor.

"You, sir, are a fascist and a bastard!" the commissar roared at me. Then he turned on his heels, led his posse out, and the panel continued. The next day the story was in most of the British papers and I had my fifteen minutes of fame, albeit as a fascist and a bastard. In that order. My name was even misspelled "Norman Spinard."

I guess it could have been worse.

Things can always get worse. One *New Worlds* fringie in those days was Sonny Mehta, a lowly genre paperback editor then, who would fuck up my career at Knopf many decades later when he had become the most powerful publishing executive in New York. "Please don't let on that you knew me when," as Bob Dylan has put it.

But that too is another out-of-sequence long story . . .

Was it easier to get published in those days, or harder? Or should I say, to make a living in SF?

It was easier to get short stories published—there were more magazines. About the same as today for genre novels, but the money was less. I mean, there was a kind of half-assed auction for *The Iron Dream*, and the winner was $3,000. I remember Larry Niven was over the moon when Ballantine raised the advance for his next novel from $1,500 to $1,750! And Niven was a Doheny heir.

You have certainly stuck it out. Would you be drawn to the field as it is today?

Early on, Harlan Ellison gave me some good advice. "You're a writer," he said, "and some of what you write is going to be SF, but write all sorts of things, whatever you can—science fiction, mainstream fiction, journalism, scripts, whatever may present itself." So for most of my career, I haven't relied totally on SF to make a living. I've written TV scripts (*Star Trek*, as everyone knows), feature films, all sorts of journalism. I wrote a monthly column for *Knight* magazine, a *Playboy* knock-off, which covered my rent. I was a regular weekly film critic and political columnist for the *Los Angeles Free Press*, which paid very little, but more or less covered the rest of my monthly nut at the time. More recently, I've written the prose in art show catalogs. Still write regular literary criticism. Just finished a stage play adaptation of *Greenhouse Summer*, first such thing I've ever tried.

I guess Harlan knows whereof he speaks, although I doubt he could match you in eclecticity. Is that a word?

I guess now it is. That's something I also learned from my dad's stories about finding work in the Great Depression. If there was a job of any kind open, he'd go for it. He'd tell 'em, Yeah, sure, I know how to do that. If he'd been offered a gig as a brain surgeon he'd probably have bought *Brain Surgery for Dummies* and given it a try if he could bullshit them into hiring him.

I've also written a number of so-called mainstream novels that were published as such—*Passing Through the Flame*, *The Mind Game*, *Pictures at 11*. And two historical novels, *The Druid King* and *Mexica*. Songs, too, which haven't earned me much money. All sorts of things except rubber checks. Never bounced a check and "eclecticity" is probably a big reason why.

But what about SF itself? Would you be drawn to the field as it is today, if you were just starting out?

The "field" as it is today—I assume by that you mean the SF publishing situation. Which sucks, literarily and economically too. SF probably wouldn't attract me as strongly as it did in the Sixties. Besides, these days, if I was writing the same kind of fiction and had never been pigeonholed as an "SF writer," I'd have a much better chance of getting my work published as general fiction. In France, that's how my more recent novels are being published.

But in an alternate universe where I was starting all over again, I'd still be writing more speculative fiction than anything else. I'd have written and would continue to write the same things that I've written, am writing, and will continue to write. Literarily, politically, no regrets. No retreat, baby, no surrender.

Speaking of France, you've lived in Paris longer than in New York, your original briar patch. How did that come about? How does a kid from the Bronx become not only a Parisian but a player in the arts and literary scene there?

Way back in the 1970s in Los Angeles, I got a call from Peter Fitting, an academic interested in SF, who told me that Richard Pinhas, a French musician who had named his band Heldon after the fictitious country in *The Iron Dream* and his wife Agnetta were coming through LA and wanted to meet me.

I said okay, but not without some trepidation on the part of myself and Dona, since fans of *The Iron Dream* might turn out to be neo-Nazis. They didn't. Instead they became friends, close friends for decades.

After Dona and I moved back to New York, and eventually broke up for several decades, I was Guest of Honor at a major SF conference in Metz.

I discovered that I had a literary and political reputation in France thanks to the French publication of *Bug Jack Barron*. So I did radio and TV in my primitive French, made more friends, etc. And started going to France for weeks at a time.

During one of those trips, my musician friend Richard—who just about *invented* electronic rock and ambient computer music before he or any other musicians even had computers—asked me to write a simple lyric and record two cuts as a singer on his forthcoming album *East/ West*.

I told him I was no singer. He told me not to worry, I would sing through a vocoder. So in France, I became a cyborged singer, which much later became the inspiration for *Little Heroes*.

Much later, I visited Paris on vacation with my then wife, novelist N. Lee Wood. She had never been to France, and we both fell in love with the city. I had long fantasized about living in Paris but was reluctant to move there alone. But now was the time to do it.

This was early-to-mid Glasnost days, and I was inspired to get a contract to write *Russian Spring*, which despite the title is largely set in Paris, and I spent a year there writing it. By the time the novel was finished (after a trip to Moscow, which despite the title, we had to do in the Russian winter) the Berlin Wall was coming down, and we were culturally connected and decided to stay.

Lee and I eventually divorced, and I decided to stay in France where I was a literary lion, half-assed not-quite-rock star, occasional political commentator, sometime screenwriter, and eventually even involved in the gallery and museum art scene, writing exhibition catalog copy. Invited to literary and SF events all over Europe.

Like Utopiales, in Nantes. It was a treat for me to get to rub shoulders with European SF legends like you and Brian Aldiss and Christopher Priest.

And bend elbows as well. The French tradition of the open literary bar helps.

Eventually I reconnected with Dona Sadock, who lived with me in Paris for two years or so after 9/11 (which we experienced pretty damn close in New York City) until real estate and monetary complications forced our exile to New York, where we now live together as I write this.

But we still spend three or four months a year in France.

Wouldn't you?

To quote Dylan again, "Honey, do you have to ask?"

In your famous Woody Allen interview (in which he ends up interviewing you!) you said you felt more "culturally connected" in France. Is that because they have the crazy idea that SF is actually Literature?

Partly, I suppose, it's because my writings are considered literature, not SF in general. But it goes deeper than that. In France, literature, art, and film are more culturally central than in the U.S. Every little village wants to do some event that puts it on the cultural map, and is willing to spend money to do it. The French Ministry of Culture, combined with the Foreign Ministry, has sent me to Mexico and New Caledonia, in effect as a cultural emissary of France, not the USA. The French Consulate in New Orleans was a great help to me and my video biographer Ben Abrass in doing research for my novel *Police State*.

I wrote a commissioned article for *Le Monde* about all this, called "The French Exception." When there were commercial negotiations between the U.S. and the French, Hollywood kept insisting that France's subsidy of its film industry violated "free trade" rules. The French in effect told them to get stuffed. Because film is an art, a part of the national cultural patrimony, and any civilized country of course must regard that as more important than mere commerce.

And France still sticks to that position.

The U.S. doesn't even have a Ministry of Culture. It has "endowments" of the arts and of the humanities (NEA, NEH).

And neither is a cabinet position. All that makes a difference. As I think I more or less said in the Woody Allen dialog, when you're a writer in France and you walk into a bank, you're at least an artist if not a celebrity. When you're a writer who walks into a bank in the U.S., you're an unemployed bum.

Speaking of unemployed bums, you have been president of SFWA (Science Fiction and Fantasy Writers of America) twice, and also president of World SF. And you were a Guest of Honor at Worldcon in 2013. Does all this mean that you have a political as well as literary agenda? Are there changes you want to see made in the way writers are treated (or treat themselves)?

Well, being Guest of Honor at a Worldcon, or for that matter at any SF convention, and being on panels and such, I don't regard as having a political agenda. That sort of thing is literary on the one hand, and PR or promotional on another—and of philosophical, scientific, personal interest on yet another, if we can allow three hands.

In SF three hands are allowed.

But being president of anything is, of course, *ipso facto* a political role, and therefore to one degree or another, successful or not, involves championing some sort of "polit-ical agenda"—though not necessarily what the French call "politique politicienne," meaning more or less party poli-tics or pursuit of a political career. My agenda was mostly about making writers' associations more professional.

But while I'm being French about it, I do admit to being "*engagé*" as a writer. That's hard to define in English; it sort of means the opposite of "apolitical," meaning that I, or at least my characters, often do have their political agendas, which I may or may not agree with, and the sto-ries can and do sometimes turn on specific political con-flicts—the outcomes of which can and usually do reflect my own political stance on the matters at issue.

However, I try not to be didactic when writing fic-tion. When I want to address political matters, I do so directly, as in "The Abnormal New Normal" in this very book. And I think doing that keeps me from turning my fiction into political screeds.

Finally, I, like any other writer, am also a citizen of something; and as a citizen, I've been politically engaged since I was maybe as young as six or seven. My family was politically engaged to the point where mornings were spent in an intricate dance of getting done in the bath-room, eating breakfast, and passing around the morning newspaper, then talking about it over breakfast, schedules permitting, so that the kids and the adults could start the day up-to-date on the news.

From a Democrat or Republican perspective?

Labor, all the way. I was told early on that ladies and gentlemen do not cross picket lines unless they have a damn good exceptional reason. And when at the age of no more than seven, when I asked Jimmy Hauser, a virtual uncle and committed Communist, for something that would give me an overall picture, he handed me H.G. Wells's *Outline of History*.

One more question. As a New Yorker, born and raised, how do you like the city these days?

Not so much. I don't like being in New York, first because it feels isolated from the wider and more diverse worlds of Europe. I don't like being in New York because it's the capital of the U.S. publishing industry, which has pretty much blackballed me for nearly a decade, resulting in four novels published or being published in France, but none in the USA. And after fifteen years in France, I have many more friends there than remain in New York. New York is also monstrously expensive to live in.

As the song goes "If you can make it there, you can make it anywhere." But doesn't that mean that it's easier to make it anywhere else?

BIBLIOGRAPHY

Series

Second Starfaring Age
1. *The Void Captain's Tale* (1982)
2. *Child of Fortune* (1985)

Novels

The Solarians (1966)
Agent of Chaos (1967)
The Men in the Jungle (1967)
Bug Jack Barron (1969)
The Iron Dream (1972)
Passing through the Flame (1975)
Riding the Torch (1978)
A World Between (1979)
The Mind Game (1980)
Songs from the Stars (1980)

The Mind Game (1983)
Little Heroes (1987)
Russian Spring (1991)
The Children of Hamelin (1991)
Deus X (1992)
Vampire Junkies (1994)
Pictures at Eleven (1994)
Journal of the Plague Years (1995)
Greenhouse Summer (1998)
He Walked Among Us (2003)
The Druid King (2003)
Mexica (2005)
Osama the Gun (2010)
Welcome to Your Dreamtime (2012)
Police State (2014)

Collections

The Last Hurrah of the Golden Horde (1970)
*Threads of Time: Three Original Novellas of Science
    Fiction* (1974) (with Gregory Benford and
    Clifford D. Simak)
No Direction Home (1975)
The Star-Spangled Future (1979)
Other Americas (1988)
Deus X and Other Stories (2003)

Anthologies edited by Spinrad

The New Tomorrows (1971)
Modern Science Fiction (1974)

Nonfiction

Staying Alive: A Writer's Guide (1983)
Experiment Perilous: Three Essays on Science Fiction (1983)
  (with Alfred Bester and Marion Zimmer Bradley)
Science Fiction in the Real World (1990)

Anthologies containing stories by Spinrad

Dangerous Visions 3 (1967)
One Hundred Years of Science Fiction (1968)
Best SF Stories from New Worlds (1969)
The Best Science Fiction of the Year (1972)
Nova 3 (1973)
Nebula Award Stories 9 (1974)
The Best of Analog (1978)
*Countdown to Midnight: Twelve Great Stories about
  Nuclear War* (1984)
Full Spectrum (1988)
Full Spectrum 3 (1991)
The Oxford Book of Science Fiction Stories (1992)
The Playboy Book of Science Fiction (1998)
Year's Best SF 4 (1999)

Short Stories

"The Last of the Romany" (1963)
"The Equalizer" (1964)
"The Ersatz Ego" (1964)
"Outward Bound" (1964)
"The Rules of the Road" (1964)
"Subjectivity" (1964)
"A Child of Mind" (1965)
"Deathwatch" (1965)
"The Age of Invention" (1966)
"Technicality" (1966)
"Carcinoma Angels" (1967)
"It's a Bird! It's a Plane!" (1967)
"A Night in Elf Hill" (1968)
"The Big Flash" (1969) Nebula nominee
"The Conspiracy" (1969)
"Dead End" (1969)
"The Entropic Gang Bang Caper" (1969)
"Heroes Die But Once" (1969)
"The Last Hurrah of the Golden Horde" (1969)
"Once More, with Feeling" (1969)
"The Lost Continent" (1970)
"Neutral Ground" (1970)
"The Weed of Time" (1970)
"No Direction Home" (1971)
"Heirloom" (1972)
"All the Sounds of the Rainbow" (1973)
"The National Pastime" (1973)

"A Thing of Beauty" (1973) Nebula nominee
"In the Eye of the Storm" (1974)
"Riding the Torch" (1974) Hugo nominee
"Save the Giant Flying Vampire Toad" (1980)
"Journals of the Plague Years" (1988) Hugo and Nebula
        nominee
"The Helping Hand" (1991)
"The Year of the Mouse" (1998)
"A Man of the Theatre" (2005)
"The Brown Revolution" (2008)
"Where No Man Pursueth" (2010)
"The Silver Bullet and the Golden Goose" (2010)
"Out There" (2011)
"Far Distant Suns" (2013)

THE AUTHOR IN 199 WORDS

NORMAN SPINRAD HAS BEEN a radio talk show host, songwriter, performer, recording artist, literary agent, president of a couple of writers' organizations, underground journalist, film critic, political commentator, blogger, literary critic, art commentator, world traveler, and interviewer. He cooks quite a bit and rather well, and is a pretty good photographer, a pretty lousy painter, and a somewhat better sculptor.

In addition to these interests he has, over a half century, managed to find time to write several television scripts, two produced feature films (screwed up by would-be auteur directors), a book of literary criticism, a book of collected political essays, a book of practical advice to writers, and is slowly working on a cookbook.

In addition, he has written twenty some odd novels, including *Bug Jack Barron*, *The Iron Dream*, *Songs from the Stars*, *The Void Captain's Tale*, *He Walked Among Us*, *Russian Spring*, *Pictures at 11*, *Mexica*, *Osama the Gun*, *Welcome to Your Dreamtime, Police State, The Men in the Jungle, Agent of Chaos, Passing through the Flame, The Children of Hamelin, Greenhouse Summer,* and *Child of Fortune,* and sixty or seventy short stories translated into something like twenty languages, not all of which have been identified.

PM PRESS
OUTSPOKEN AUTHORS

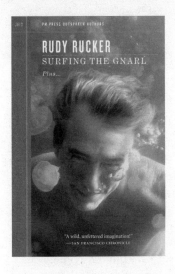

Surfing the Gnarl
Rudy Rucker
128 Pages
$12.00

The original "Mad Professor" of Cyberpunk, Rudy Rucker (along with fellow outlaws William Gibson and Bruce Sterling) transformed modern science fiction, tethering the "gnarly" speculations of quantum physics to the noir sensibilities of a skeptical and disenchanted generation. In acclaimed novels like *Wetware* and *The Hacker and the Ant* he mapped a neotopian future that belongs not to sober scientists but to drug-addled, sex-crazed youth. And won legions of fans doing it.

In his outrageous new *Surfing the Gnarl*, Dr. Rucker infiltrates fundamentalist Virginia to witness the apocalyptic clash between Bible-thumpers and Saucer Demons at a country club barbecue; undresses in orbit to explore the future of foreplay in freefall ("Rapture in Space"); and (best of all!) dons the robe of a Transreal Lifestyle Adviser with How-to Tips on how you can manipulate the Fourth Dimension to master everyday tasks like finding an apartment, dispatching a tiresome lover, organizing closets and iPods, and remaking Reality.

You'll never be the same. Is that good or bad? Your call.

PM PRESS
OUTSPOKEN AUTHORS

Report from Planet Midnight
Nalo Hopkinson
128 Pages
$12.00

Nalo Hopkinson has been busily (and wonderfully) "subverting the genre" since her first novel, *Brown Girl in the Ring*, won a Locus Award for SF and Fantasy in 1999. Since then she has acquired a prestigious World Fantasy Award, a legion of adventurous and aware fans, a reputation for intellect seasoned with humor, and a place of honor in the short list of SF writers who are tearing down the walls of category and transporting readers to previously unimagined planets and realms.

Never one to hold her tongue, Hopkinson takes on sexism and racism in publishing ("Report from Planet Midnight") in a historic and controversial presentation to her colleagues and fans.

Plus . . .

"Message in a Bottle," a radical new twist on the time travel tale that demolishes the sentimental myth of childhood innocence; and "Shift," a tempestuous erotic adventure in which Caliban gets the girl. Or does he?

And Featuring: our Outspoken Interview, an intimate one-on-one that delivers a wealth of insight, outrage, irreverence, and top-secret Caribbean spells.

PM PRESS
OUTSPOKEN AUTHORS

*The Great Big Beautiful
Tomorrow*
Cory Doctorow
144 Pages
$12.00

Cory Doctorow burst on the SF scene in 2000 like a rocket, inspiring awe in readers (and envy in other writers) with his bestselling novels and stories, which he insisted on giving away via Creative Commons. Meanwhile, as coeditor of the wildly popular blog Boing Boing, he became the radical new voice of the Web, boldly arguing for internet freedom from corporate control.

Doctorow's activism and artistry are both on display in this Outspoken Author edition. The crown jewel is his novella, *The Great Big Beautiful Tomorrow*, the high-velocity adventures of a transhuman teenager in a toxic post-Disney dystopia, battling wireheads and wumpuses (and having fun doing it!) until he meets the "meat girl" of his dreams, and is forced to choose between immortality and sex.

Plus . . .

A live transcription of Cory's historic address to the 2010 World SF Convention, "Creativity vs. Copyright," dramatically presenting his controversial case for open-source in both information and art.

Also included is an international Outspoken Interview (skyped from England, Canada, and the U.S.) in which Doctorow reveals the surprising sources of his genius.

PM PRESS
OUTSPOKEN AUTHORS

The Science of Herself
Karen Joy Fowler
128 Pages
$12.00

Widely respected in the so-called "mainstream" for her *New York Times* bestselling novels, Karen Joy Fowler is also a formidable, often controversial, and always exuberant presence in Science Fiction. Here she debuts a provocative new story written especially for this series. Set in the days of Darwin, "The Science of Herself" is a marvelous hybrid of SF and historical fiction: the almost-true story of England's first female paleontologist who took on the Victorian old-boy establishment armed with only her own fierce intelligence—and an arsenal of dino bones.

Plus...

"The Pelican Bar," a homely tale of family ties that makes Guantánamo look like summer camp; "The Further Adventures of the Invisible Man," a droll tale of sports, shoplifting and teen sex; and "The Motherhood Statement," a quietly angry upending of easy assumptions that shows off Fowler's deep radicalism and impatience with conservative homilies and liberal pieties alike.

And Featuring: our Outspoken Interview in which Fowler prophesies California's fate, reveals the role of bad movies in good marriages, and intimates that girls just want to have fun (which means make trouble).

PM PRESS
OUTSPOKEN AUTHORS

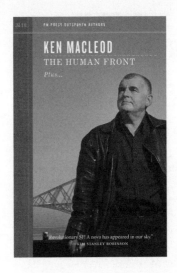

The Human Front
Ken MacLeod
128 Pages
$12.00

Ken MacLeod is one of the brightest and most progressive of Britain's "Hard SF" stars who navigate exciting new futures to the delight of legions of fans around the world. His works combine cutting-edge scientific speculation, socialist and anarchist themes, and a deeply humanistic vision. Described by fans and adversaries alike as a "techno-utopian socialist," MacLeod thrusts his characters into uncanny encounters that have included AI singularities, divergent human evolution, and posthuman cyborg-resurrection.

In his novella *The Human Front*, a young Scottish guerrilla fighter is drawn into low-intensity sectarian war in a high-intensity dystopian future, and the arrival of an alien intruder (complete with saucer!) calls for new tactics and strange alliances. Its companion piece, "Other Deviations," first published in this edition, reveals the complex origins of MacLeod's alternate history.

Plus . . .

"The Future Will Happen Here, Too," in which a Hebridean writer celebrates the landscapes that shaped his work, measures Scotland's past against humanity's future, and peers into the eyes of an eel.

And Featuring: our irreverent Outspoken Interview, a candid and often cantankerous conversation that showcases our author's deep erudition and mordant wit.

"Shirley serves up the bloody heart of a sick and rotting society with the aplomb of an Aztec surgeon on Dexedrine."
—BOOKLIST

PM PRESS
OUTSPOKEN AUTHORS

New Taboos
John Shirley
128 Pages
$12.00

Mixing outlaw humor, SF adventure, and cutting social criticism, Shirley draws upon his entire arsenal of narrative and commentary. The title essay, "New Taboos" is his prescription for a radical revisioning of America. A new novella, *A State of Imprisonment*, is a horrifying and grimly hilarious look at the privatization of the prison industry. "Why We Need Forty Years of Hell," Shirley's 2011 TEDx address, presents his proudly contrarian view of the near future.

Also featured is our Outspoken Interview showcasing the author's transgressive sensibility, deep humanity, and mordant wit.

"Astonishingly consistent and rigorously horrifying. All his stories give off the chill of top-grade horror."
—*New York Times*

PM PRESS
OUTSPOKEN AUTHORS

The Wild Girls
Ursula K. Le Guin
112 Pages
$12.00

Ursula K. Le Guin is the one modern science fiction author who truly needs no introduction. In the forty years since *The Left Hand of Darkness*, her works have changed not only the face but the tone and the agenda of SF, introducing themes of gender, race, socialism, and anarchism, all the while thrilling readers with trips to strange (and strangely familiar) new worlds. She is our exemplar of what fantastic literature can and should be about.

Her Nebula winner *The Wild Girls*, newly revised and presented here in book form for the first time, tells of two captive "dirt children" in a society of sword and silk, whose determination to enter "that possible even when unattainable space in which there is room for justice" leads to a violent and loving end.

Plus . . .

Le Guin's scandalous and scorching *Harper's* essay, "Staying Awake While We Read," (also collected here for the first time) which demolishes the pretensions of corporate publishing and the basic assumptions of capitalism as well. And of course our Outspoken Interview, which promises to reveal the hidden dimensions of America's best-known SF author. And delivers.

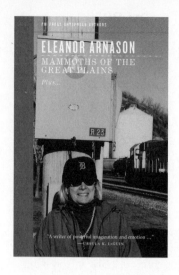

"A writer of powerful imagination and emotion ..."
—URSULA K. LeGUIN

PM PRESS
OUTSPOKEN AUTHORS

Mammoths of the Great Plains
Eleanor Arnason
152 Pages
$12.00

When President Thomas Jefferson sent Lewis and Clark to explore the West, he told them to look especially for mammoths. Jefferson had seen bones and tusks of the great beasts in Virginia, and he suspected—he hoped!—that they might still roam the Great Plains. In Eleanor Arnason's imaginative alternate history, they do: shaggy herds thunder over the grasslands, living symbols of the oncoming struggle between the Native peoples and the European invaders. And in an unforgettable saga that soars from the badlands of the Dakotas to the icy wastes of Siberia, from the Russian Revolution to the AIM protests of the 1960s, Arnason tells of a modern woman's struggle to use the weapons of DNA science to fulfill the ancient promises of her Lakota heritage.

Plus . . .

"Writing SF During World War III," and an Outspoken Interview that takes you straight into the heart and mind of one of today's edgiest and most uncompromising speculative authors.

> "Eleanor Arnason nudges both human and natural history
> around so gently in this tale that you hardly know you're
> not in the world-as-we-know-it until you're quite at
> home in a North Dakota where you've never been before,
> listening to your grandmother tell you the world."
> —Ursula K. Le Guin

FRIENDS OF

These are indisputably momentous times—the financial system is melting down globally and the Empire is stumbling. Now more than ever there is a vital need for radical ideas.

In the six years since its founding—and on a mere shoestring—PM Press has risen to the formidable challenge of publishing and distributing knowledge and entertainment for the struggles ahead. With over 250 releases to date, we have published an impressive and stimulating array of literature, art, music, politics, and culture. Using every available medium, we've succeeded in connecting those hungry for ideas and information to those putting them into practice.

Friends of PM allows you to directly help impact, amplify, and revitalize the discourse and actions of radical writers, filmmakers, and artists. It provides us with a stable foundation from which we can build upon our early successes and provides a much-needed subsidy for the materials that can't necessarily pay their own way. You can help make that happen—and receive every new title automatically delivered to your door once a month—by joining as a Friend of PM Press. And, we'll throw in a free T-shirt when you sign up.

Here are your options:

- $30 a month: Get all books and pamphlets plus 50% discount on all webstore purchases
- $40 a month: Get all PM Press releases (including CDs and DVDs) plus 50% discount on all webstore purchases
- $100 a month: Superstar—Everything plus PM merchandise, free downloads, and 50% discount on all webstore purchases

For those who can't afford $30 or more a month, we're introducing Sustainer Rates at $15, $10, and $5. Sustainers get a free PM Press T-shirt and a 50% discount on all purchases from our website.

Your Visa or Mastercard will be billed once a month, until you tell us to stop. Or until our efforts succeed in bringing the revolution around. Or the financial meltdown of Capital makes plastic redundant. Whichever comes first.

PM Press was founded at the end of 2007 by a small collection of folks with decades of publishing, media, and organizing experience. PM Press co-conspirators have published and distributed hundreds of books, pamphlets, CDs, and DVDs. Members of PM have founded enduring book fairs, spearheaded victorious tenant organizing campaigns, and worked closely with bookstores, academic conferences, and even rock bands to deliver political and challenging ideas to all walks of life. We're old enough to know what we're doing and young enough to know what's at stake.

We seek to create radical and stimulating fiction and non-fiction books, pamphlets, t-shirts, visual and audio materials to entertain, educate, and inspire you. We aim to distribute these through every available channel with every available technology—whether that means you are seeing anarchist classics at our bookfair stalls; reading our latest vegan cookbook at the café; downloading geeky fiction e-books; or digging new music and timely videos from our website.

PM Press is always on the lookout for talented and skilled volunteers, artists, activists, and writers to work with. If you have a great idea for a project or can contribute in some way, please get in touch.

PM Press
PO Box 23912
Oakland CA 94623
510-658-3906
www.pmpress.org